Storm

Savage Brotherhood MC: Book Eight

A Paranormal Romance

by Jasmine Wylder

Table of Contents

Chapter One

Storm

Daniel stood near the back of the room as everybody partied, danced and drank around him. He had a beer in one hand to stop people from asking him if he wanted anything, but he didn't take so much as a sip. It was a joyous occasion, he knew that, but he wasn't much in the mood for celebrating. His uncle, Stewart, and his new wife, Frieda, were at the center of the dance floor, making out. A wedding ought to be happier than this, but Daniel couldn't shake the frustration and disappointment.

It wasn't that he wasn't happy for Stewart and Frieda. He was. They had gone through a lot to get to this point and deserved their happily ever after. What was frustrating was that they had decided to move to Frieda's house. Daniel had just moved into the apartment Stewart was living in, relieved to have finally convinced his parents that it was safe enough for him to live with his uncle.

With this development, they were both talking about him moving back to the vampire kingdom his mother ruled.

It wasn't that Daniel didn't see their point. Although he had grown and matured from infancy to adulthood in a year, it was hard for them to let him go. He was their miracle baby, half-vampire, half-shifter. With his mother's position as queen and with shifters and vampires alike disgusted that he even existed, it was dangerous for him. So, it was doubly hard for his parents to let him go when they knew the threats out here.

But he was a grown man. Maybe he'd just celebrated his first birthday not long ago, but that didn't mean he was any less a man. People would think he was his father's younger brother looking at them. Many people, after talking with him, assumed he was *older* than his father, even. Daniel didn't want to put his parents through unnecessary fear, but the fact was... he was a grown man and they weren't able to see him that way. He needed to start seeing more of the world outside of the vampire kingdom.

He needed to live his *life*. He'd been working with the alpha of the Savage Brotherhood, a motorcycle club, to get his fighting skills up to par, but he needed more practical application in relationships, meeting new people... he wasn't going to be able to do that if he stayed home all his life.

He glanced around, finding his mother in the crowd. Guinevere would be the harder sell, since she had gone centuries thinking she would never be able to have a child. She looked distracted, unsettled. Did she suspect what he was going to say, that he didn't intend on moving back?

With a sigh, Daniel took a gulp of his beer. No time like the present... He started heading over to her. Just when he reached her, though, Guinevere let out a pained cry. She fell to one knee, an arm wrapped around her abdomen. Daniel's heart jumped to his throat as he rushed to his mother's side. His father, Andy, was at her other side in a heartbeat.

Stewart and Frieda approached, looking concerned, and someone turned off the music. “What’s going on?”

Guinevere’s fingers dug into the carpet. Sweat broke over her pale face, and Daniel grasped her arm. “Mom?”

“Gwen, look at me,” Andy plead. “What’s happening?”

“Did she drink too much shifter blood?” somebody in the crowd asked.

Daniel glanced around helplessly as Guinevere cried out in pain again. Agony twisted her face as she panted. He gripped her arm tightly but didn’t know what to do. His heart pounded shallowly, and the familiar feeling of his wolf rose in his chest, just out of reach; it had been getting stronger since he left the vampire kingdom, but he hadn’t yet been able to shift.

"Mom," he pled.

Guinevere's sweat-slick face turned to him. Her eyes rolled wildly, unable to focus on him. Her jaw was clenched so tight her small fangs bit into her lip, causing blood to trickle down her chin. She opened her mouth, gasped, and grasped his arm.

"Daniel," she choked out. "I'm sorry... I'm so sorry... the Master has returned. Can you feel it?"

Daniel's eyes widened. "The Master?"

He'd only heard rumors, the name whispered in fear. What was she talking about?

"He calls for us," her face contorted with agony again and she dropped to the floor. "He calls for us to obey his will. Destroy his enemies. But I won't! I can't... Andy—"

"I'm here," Andy said, wrapping his arms around her. "I'm not leaving you."

Guinevere let out an inhuman shriek—and then whipped around, her fingernails like claws as they struck across Andy's face. He let out a howl of pain and surprise as he recoiled. Guinevere's hands wrapped around his neck and Daniel seized her around the waist, dragging her back. Tears streamed down Guinevere's face as she sobbed out a single word.

"Run."

Daniel tightened his hold around his mother's waist as she writhed in his grasp, hands still reaching out for Andy.

Andy was there, his eyes wide in fear and betrayal.

"I can't fight him," Guinevere shouted. "I can't resist his commands. Run! Please! Before I—"

She choked off her words; at that moment, the doors burst open. A flood of vampires poured into the small space. Daniel let out a strangled shout as his grip on Guinevere loosened. She tore from his grasp and lunged for Andy even as Daniel tried to grab her again. A vampire's packed fist struck him across the temple and Daniel tumbled back, quickly moving to defend himself blindly. His feet lashed out, catching a vampire in the stomach and pushing him back.

Daniel rolled to his feet to find a gun pointed right at his face. He tensed, gazing past the gun to see it was Mildred, one of his mother's handmaids and one of the women who was always there when he was growing up. Tears streaked down her face and with a plummeting heart, he knew she couldn't control herself, either.

Glancing around, all the vampires now engaged in fighting the shifters were friends, allies. And all had looks of utter devastation on their faces.

"I don't have to kill you," Mildred whispered. "You're different, you have not shifted. Please don't make me kill you."

Her voice broke as Guinevere let out a cry of pain. Daniel's head whipped around to see her fists driving into Andy's face and chest while he tried to defend himself without hurting his wife.

Daniel's hands moved without him even having to think, knocking aside Mildred's gun. It went off, the bullet hitting another vampire in the shoulder. She let out a cry as Daniel grabbed her wrist, twisted the gun from her hand and drove a fist into her stomach. His own stomach twisted with pain and regret, but he couldn't afford to let himself stop.

With a few quick twists, he popped Mildred's arms from her sockets, sending screams from her throat but preventing her from hurting anybody. He lowered her gently to the floor, face twisted in apology, and lunged for his mother, whose fangs were lengthening as they inched towards Andy's throat.

Before he reached her, a half dozen more shifters poured into the room. The space was so tightly packed that it was difficult for any of them to move, much less fight. Guinevere was jostled to one side as Typhoon, in his huge wolf's form, batted vampires aside left and right. But more vampires were coming, strange vampires with a bloodlust bright in their eyes.

Daniel fought as hard as he could. He twisted arms from their sockets, broke legs, rammed his skull into noses; his skin was cut open by tooth and claw, his blood filled the air. And then a strong fist drove into his kidneys, driving him to his knees. As darkness swirled in front of his vision, Typhoon's familiar scent curled into his nostrils.

Confusion whirled in his head; why was Typhoon attacking *him*? But the fists continued to rain down on him, and Daniel stopped trying to reason it out—he fought back, throwing Typhoon off him briefly before the alpha was on him again.

And then, a cold, clear voice rang out over them all.

“Enough.”

A final fist rammed into Daniel’s face. Typhoon had him by the throat, face twisted as he panted. Sweat broke over his face and with a thrill of horror, Daniel realized what was happening. Typhoon was half vampire, like him. And the Master was able to control vampires… even Typhoon, it seemed.

Yet Daniel didn’t feel any obligations to attack the other shifters; he was half vamp, too…

Typhoon jerked him up by his collar and forced him to his knees. Around them, all the vampires were holding the shifters down in similar positions. A few of them looked joyous, but most were just afraid. In through the door strode the biggest, meanest looking vampire Daniel had ever seen. He was easily seven feet tall, with shoulders so broad he had to turn sideways to get through the door. His eyes were blood-red as he glanced over the subjected shifters and grinned.

"Your master has returned," he breathed, opening his arms wide. "I am Apep, your god, and it is well that you worship me. I created you from the dust, and it is well that I have returned when I have. Vampires trodden under the feet of beast and men? This shall not do. You are my slaves, you filthy beasts, and you will learn to do as I command."

Apep. Daniel growled low in his throat. Guinevere had made sure he knew about his people's history; Apep was supposedly the first vampire, a god in his time.

The noise got the vampire's attention, and he stalked over but didn't look at Daniel. Instead, Apep put a thick digit beneath Typhoon's chin and made him look up. "You have the stench of the shifters but the bloodlust of a vampire. How crude, a bastard hybrid. You will be useful to me, anyway."

Typhoon let out a choked snarl. Apep's eyes hardened and his lip lifted, revealing a single fang.

"A fighter? Well, I will simply have to break the beast's spirit, won't I? Kiss my foot."

He proffered one of his feet toward Typhoon. He snarled, sweat making his hands clammy, but, as though a giant hand was manipulating his actions, he bent and kissed the foot. Daniel's chest heaved, but he felt no need to obey the commands Apep was giving—and Typhoon's sweaty grip on him was failing.

Daniel ripped himself free of Typhoon and struck Apep in the throat. The giant vampire stumbled back, a surprised look coming to his face, but Daniel didn't take the time to let that stop him. As the vampires released their shifters and surged to block his path to Apep, he turned on his heel. He grabbed the arm of his aunt, Roxy, and shoved her toward the door. Her husband, Josef, scrambled after her, shielding her with his body, as several of the vampires lifted guns.

Bullets whistled through the air. Bursts of blood and gunpowder filled the air. Daniel didn't stop moving, dragging shifters to their feet and shoving them to doors or windows, anywhere he could to get them out.

The last was his father. His hand was outstretched toward Guinevere as Typhoon remained on his knees next to Apep. Their eyes were wide with horror, and Daniel knew he had no choice. He seized his father and drove him toward the window. Andy shouted, Guinevere called out—and then they tumbled out the window together, falling two stories to land heavily on the ground.

"Guinevere," Andy gasped out, trying to shove his son off.

"If you go back, he'll make her kill you!" Daniel tightened his grip. "Don't put us through that, Dad. Please."

Andy snarled, but his movements became jerky.

Daniel dragged him to his feet and limped toward where Frieda and Stewart stood. They had to get to the other shifters. Put out a warning to the Brotherhood—Apep had returned, and everything was going to hell.

Chapter Two

Gracie

Gracie Underhill, 12:45.

The appointment card was crumpled and damp with sweat. Gracie stared at it again, her stomach twisting into knots as she stepped off the bus into the heart of Ivywood's downtown. The large city hall, a building made rich with history that Gracie used to adore seeing, now loomed like a deathtrap. Which, in many ways, it was.

It had been only a few months since her life had been turned upside down. Tears streaked down her face as she saw the same fear on other young women heading for the city hall. Three months ago, she thought vampires and shifters were stuff out of corny romance novels. She never understood the appeal of the supernatural.

And then vampires had revealed themselves to the world. They'd toppled governments, destroyed the military, and made human beings their slaves. Since then, fifty women were gathered at city hall on the first of every month. Five were chosen—for what, nobody knew, but they were never seen again. The cards came in the mail, telling the women when to gather, what to wear, and a list of questions to prepare answers for.

Gracie knew that her turn was coming up. When she had gotten the card in the mail, she had sat down and wept. She had considered simply not showing up, packing up the bare essentials and taking off. But the stories of what happened to the other women who'd tried that haunted her. Their families imprisoned, the women themselves taken up to the palaces where their new vampire overlords lived.

She didn't have a family, and her friends were few and far between, but Gracie didn't want to think about what they would do to punish her if she tried to run. If she went to the choosing, then there was a chance she wasn't going to be chosen. If she tried to run, they'd find her and drag her away. Better go and take the chance she might be able to go home again.

Her breathing was shallow, and her hands were cold as she climbed the stairs to the city hall. The other women were crying, just as she was, although there were one or two that looked eager—whispering to each other that the chosen women were taken as vampire brides and made into vampires themselves. Gracie shook her head as she walked past them to the reception desk, where a hard-faced vampire woman sat. How could anybody find this exciting?

"Take the elevator to the top floor," the vampire woman said without even looking at her. "You'll be taken to the examination rooms from there."

Gracie's legs trembled, and her throat was dry, but she managed to nod and head for the elevators. Inside, a woman clutched a blanket to her chest, sobbing openly. It was a baby blanket—was she a young mother, facing the possibility of never seeing her child again? Gracie turned her face away, wanting to give some words of comfort but finding nothing to say.

Out of the elevator, there were several more female vampires waiting. One of them took her by the arm and pulled her silently down the hall, to a cool room where she was told to strip off her clothing. Gracie held in a sob as she did so, wondering what sort of things would happen. To her surprise, the vampire gave her a hospital robe to wear and then did a checkup similar to one that she'd receive at the doctor's office.

"What will happen to me if I'm chosen?" she breathed out, daring to ask. If she was braver, perhaps she'd attack this vampire, try to fight her way free. Or perhaps try to ensure she was chosen, and then blow them all to hell.

"It depends on what you're chosen for." The vampire gave her a pitying look. "You will not be killed. Strong, healthy women as yourself are too valuable a resource. But you may be used to provide blood or sex to our lords, in which case you will most likely wish you were dead... for a time, at least."

Gracie shuddered at the thought. "I'm not healthy or strong," she blurted. "I'm overweight. Don't you think that they'd rather have someone fitter?"

"Your medical records state that you are healthy. Your weight is not too high. Now please give me the answers to the questions you were given."

Gracie's heart sank, but she dutifully pulled out the question card and handed it over. The vampire took it. Her eyes widened when she saw the card, visibly shaken. Gracie stared, wanting to ask what that was about but not quite daring. The vampire quickly left the room, and Gracie waited, shivering. Moments later, she returned with a tall, thin man who looked more like a walking corpse than anything else.

"Come with me," he grumbled at her, eyes bright with curiosity.

Gracie reached for her clothes.

"You won't need those," the man grunted and grabbed her arm. "We cannot keep the master waiting."

Terror flooded her. The master—she had seen his image on TV. A huge vampire, claiming to be the Egyptian God Apep. If she had eaten anything earlier, she would have thrown it up right now. What did he want with her? She was just a struggling single in a city full of people. What could she have possibly done to receive attention from the god of all vampires?

“No,” she gasped out, beginning to struggle against his hold. “No, please don’t!”

She turned back to the female vampire. Guilt was written across her face as she turned her back. Gracie punched the vampire holding her. Her mind was an utter blank as terror consumed her, her arms and legs flailing of their own accord. She screamed, writhing in the vampire’s grasp, but he didn’t seem to notice. Her blows might have been puffs of wind for all they moved him. Tears streamed down her face, and her heart beat wildly.

“I won’t,” she screamed as if words alone had the power to save her. “I won’t! I won’t!”

The vampire grunted as she managed to land a punch on his jaw. He whirled on her, eyes narrowed as he struggled to hold her. “You have no choice, girl. Besides, our master himself chose you. You should be honored. He has taken no woman since his rebirth, and he has decided that you will have the honor of belonging to him and him alone. Why fight your destiny? It could be worse.”

Gracie laughed in his face even as her knees gave out. She crumpled to the floor and hid her face, sobbing. The vampire grunted again and picked her up, letting her hang limp but with a firm grip around her middle. Images flashed through her mind of everything she feared, and her stomach rebelled. Nothing came up but a little flem, which she spat into the vampire’s face.

He ground his teeth and dragged her along.

They went to an elevator at the other end of the hallway and took it straight down to the parking beneath the hall. There, the vampire took her to a car and shoved her inside. Gracie's hand whipped out and locked the doors before the vampire could get to the other side. He glowered at her as he removed the key from his pocket.

She unlocked her door and darted through the cars, away from the vampire.

"You little—" the vampire snarled as he charged after her, swooping through the air like a bat.

The thunderous noise of a motorbike made Gracie's head whip around. She ran away from it instinctively, imagining Apep himself hurtling towards her on a Harley

Davidson. The vampire chasing her let out a hiss as his hand closed around her hair jerking her to a stop. The roaring motor grew closer until she could feel the vibrations of it in her chest. The vampire released her—something huge flew over her head and there was a strangled shout.

Gracie dove toward a van, scrambling beneath it. Four huge paws clawed the ground as the vampire howled in pain. There was a tearing noise, a cracking noise, and then silence. The vampire's body hit the cement of the garage heavily. A scent like rotten fruit filled the air as blackened blood spread out around the broken body.

The paws faced toward her. Gracie slapped both her hands over her mouth, trying to stifle her heavy breathing. The animal bent, a huge wolf's head peering below the van to gaze at her. Green eyes seemed to pierce right through her. Then, in the blink of an eye, the wolf was replaced by a man. Big, strong, with a heavy frown on his face.

"Get out from under there," he ordered. "We don't have much time before more vamps arrive. Unless you'd rather I leave you here."

A shifter. Gracie's breath caught in her throat. Like vampires, they had emerged only three months ago. They were said to be fighting the vampires in secret, although the news was full of their wicked and murderous ways.

But anything was better than being prey to a vampire. Gracie didn't let herself think about the tales of torture and rape, instead hoping that this time her roulette choice would be to her benefit. She scrambled out from under the van. The shifter picked her up easily and carried her to his idling motorcycle. He put her on, climbing on behind her.

It was only then that she registered that he was stark naked. And a very naked part of him pressed up against her from behind, and she became very aware of how flimsy the hospital gown actually was. Heat flared to her cheeks as she attempted to cover herself better, but then they were off, and it was all she could do to hold on and not get thrown from the bike.

There were shouts and howls from behind them as they tore out of the garage. Sunlight fell on Gracie's face and she sucked in a deep breath, as though it was the first air she'd breathed. The shifter's heat against her back felt solid, and she tried to thank him, but her words were snatched away by the wind.

They drove for what seemed like hours; several times they darted through alleys or down stairs unexpectedly. She was sore all over from the jostling by the time it was over. The wolf lifted her off the bike in front of a small, shabby-looking building. He picked the bike up under one arm, seized her wrist in the other, and dragged her inside.

As soon as the door slammed shut behind them, several people emerged from doorways. Roughly half of them were women, and both sexes stared at her for a moment before turning furious gazes at her rescuer.

"What the hell, Daniel?" one of the women snarled as she strode forward.

“We agreed—no unnecessary risks! Apep’s going to be on our asses for this.”

Her rescuer shrugged. “You agreed, Aunt Roxy. I said I wasn’t going to let Apep get his hands on another one. He picked her for a reason. Shouldn’t we find out that reason before letting him suck her dry?”

Gracie shrank back from the glares that they were giving her. They must all be shifters. And they didn’t want her here. The horrible thought that they might send her back flooded her and her knees buckled. Daniel caught her. Gracie shook her head, whispering pleas because her throat was too dry for any sort of volume.

“Well, we can’t send her back now,” another woman said, putting her hands on her hips. “And the charms here have protected us from the vampires this long. Come here," she held out a hand. "Let's get you dressed."

A couple of the men strode past her to glare at Daniel, but he met their gazes coolly. From their features, they were all brothers. Gracie shivered as she let herself be led away, her mind blank once more, though this time in relief. Daniel had saved her from the worst fate she could imagine—and he would always have her gratitude for that.

Chapter Three

Storm

The remnants of the Brotherhood's leadership all stared at him with looks ranging from anger to resigned acceptance. He didn't flinch from any of them, already knowing what they would say about his actions. Yes, going after Gracie was a risk, but they had figured out the secret code to find Apep's chosen weeks ago. If he didn't act to save this girl, she'd end up like the others. An empty shell cast into an incinerator.

Thunder, previous alpha of the Ivywood chapter, was the first to speak. "Well, now that Storm has gone against our wishes and grabbed the girl, we might as well figure out what Apep wants with her. She might be able to give us clues to his next plan."

"Be that as it may," Blizzard growled, leaning on the wall. "Storm needs to be punished—for going against the vote and putting us all, as well as our mates and children, at risk."

Daniel didn't let himself flinch. Blizzard had four children here, and his mate, Shadow, had been badly hurt at the last safehouse that fell to the vampires. She was recovered now, but it only made sense that his protective instincts were in a higher gear. Tornado, Shadow's bother and previous alpha of the Coalfell chapter, nodded, though his face was heavy in a frown.

"We can figure that out once we've got our next move planned. Hurricane brought back info about the Easthallow chapter being rounded up by vampires. We need to move in and find survivors—"

This time Daniel couldn't help but growl. He understood their views. All of them had been fighting vampires since they were teens; they had seen some terrible things in their times and were playing defensively until they could rebuild their strength to go after Apep's forces or rally humans into a full-out revolt.

"That's band-aids on a gut wound." Daniel narrowed his eyes at Tornado and then Blizzard. His father and uncle were standing close by, looking unhappy, but they didn't interrupt. "We can't keep rounding up survivors. We're running out of places to put them, and we'll keep losing more numbers if all we do is run and hide. We have to go for the head. The girl was Apep's chosen. We can use her to draw him out."

"And then what?" Shadow spat at him, bristling like the leopard she was. "We ask him nicely to stop? He's killed everyone who has gone after him. Some of our best alphas."

"Because they went after him alone. If we can be unified—"

"And how do you intend to get close enough to put in a blow?" Thunder glowered at him. "Sure, maybe you can shift now and maybe you have the biggest wolf I've seen since—"

He cut himself off, but they all knew what he was thinking. Since Typhoon. None of the others, except for Andy, had known he was a wolf-vampire hybrid. Finding out this way had shaken their trust in him as their alpha, especially now, since he was under Apep's control. Daniel felt his hands curling to fists. Typhoon's unwilling betrayal was another reason why Thunder and the others didn't trust him. And he knew what Shadow was going to say before she even said it.

"How do you intend on getting close enough to him without falling under his sway?" Her eyes flashed as they pierced right through him. "He can control vampires; how do we know that you won't suddenly find yourself unable to fight his control?"

Daniel ground his teeth together.

Andy spoke in a snarl. "If Daniel was going to be taken over by Apep, he would have already."

Beside him, Frieda and Stewart nodded their support.

"Regardless," Tornado broke in, stepping a little closer to his sister. "We can't get at Apep. He always has a good three dozen protectors around him, Typhoon and your mother included," he added, glancing at Daniel. "If we attacked him, we'd have to tear through his guard before we got to him. Do you want to have to kill your mother in order to kill Apep?"

Daniel glowered at him. Guinevere would rather be dead than serving the likes of Apep but the thought of her dying, of having to kill her to defend himself or get to Apep? It left his blood running cold.

When Daniel didn't respond, Tornado snorted and shook his head. "I get it. If we could take out Apep, maybe we'd be able to put this all behind us. But he's been killed before, remember?

And the vampires brought him back with their rituals and sacrifices. No. We need to protect and regroup the Brotherhood. Only when we've bound together in strength again do we have a chance against the vampires. Especially since the humans are too cowardly to do anything against them."

"And while we're doing that, our numbers dwindle and his grow!"

"I don't like all the running and hiding either," Shadow snapped. "But I agree with Jackson. We have to rebuild our strength, or we'll just be breaking against the shore. Apep is too powerful to take just because we're determined. We have to play this smart. And let's be honest, we haven't been able to hold down a single line. How could we mount an offensive?"

"You're only saying that because you're Tornado's sister and you have to agree," Josef snapped at her.

Shadow snorted. "As though you're not defending Storm's idea because he's your nephew by marriage."

Daniel sighed, rubbing his temples. They were losing focus. Again. There were so many powerful personalities here and everyone had their own ideas on how to proceed. They weren't fighting within their group so much as squabbling constantly. That, more than anything, was making it exceedingly difficult to get any real work done against the vampires.

"We don't have the manpower to go on the offensive yet," Blizzard rumbled, glaring at Josef. "You know that as well as any of us. We agreed that we need to regroup our strength. The boy's actions today, bringing Apep's chosen to us, is going to make that even more difficult."

Andy, Stewart, and Frieda all bristled. Daniel leaned against the wall, folding his arms as the three of them started to growl. Family loyalty would defend him for now, but as soon as they were alone? He imagined his father at least would have quite a few things to say about his 'heroics' today. As though it was any different than when Tornado drove into the heart of a vampire kingdom to retrieve his mate, Ava, or when Blizzard and Shadow had done the same to rescue their daughters. Both times, it had ended with the vampires coming after the Brotherhood, but when Daniel saved an innocent girl?

"Our numbers are increasingly scattered," Andy spat, his hands clenched. "Our leader is in the hands of Apep. My wife, my mate, is forced to serve him. How long are we going to wait? You talk about rebuilding our strength, but when was the last time any of you added to our numbers? We don't have time to stand around and argue!"

Tornado growled as he puffed himself up, towering over Andy. "I'm sorry for your mate, Twister. I really am. But I am not risking my mate and my children on..."

"On what?" Andy went toe-to-toe with him. "On the chance to protect them forever from the vampire threat?"

None of them noticed when Daniel slipped from the room. He wanted to shout at them all to shut up and demand that they think, actually think, and understand that taking out Apep soon was the only way to go. But, of course, they wouldn't listen. He was just the hybrid freak, the one who couldn't be trusted because he was half vampire.

Daniel headed to the room he shared with the rest of his family. The safehouse was a tiny, cramped one that could not hold everyone who was currently living in it. They had to suffice themselves to sleep in whatever nooks they found. As for privacy or personal space? It was unheard of. Curtains strung in the center of rooms were the best they could do to give each family their own space.

Ava and Mia, Typhoon's mate, sat watching their children play, talking in hushed voices. Mia glanced at him and turned her face away. Daniel's stomach twisted as he hurried to his room. Roxy was there with his cousins, but Daniel went to his bed and rolled over so his back was toward her. She didn't speak, and he was grateful for that.

Why hadn't he succumbed to Apep's control? Was it possible that Apep had left him free, as a secret weapon to pull out when needed to crush the rest of the Brotherhood? Could he be influenced by Apep without even realizing it? He hadn't thought much about rescuing Gracie Underhill... he had decided to keep with the rest of them and not do anything, and then the next thing he knew, he was driving to Ivywood.

And if Apep didn't have control or influence over him... why had he been spared and Typhoon taken? They were both hybrids, there was no reason for

Typhoon to have succumbed to Apep's control but Daniel go free.

Thinking about Typhoon only made his stomach twist tighter. He tried to turn his mind to something else, but without any luck. For the past three months, Typhoon and Guinevere had been haunting their steps. Taking out the safehouses they stayed in, attacking their warehouses. Everywhere they had supplies or could find a safe place, it wasn't long before Typhoon led a bunch of vampires to them. Daniel had seen him a handful of times, and there was a blank, defeated look on his face every single time.

Without a leader, the Brotherhood was going to fall. It was only a matter of time before things came to a head, when there would be no more running and hiding.

And now, he wished he had gotten more life experiences before being thrust headlong into this mess. Typhoon had spent a lot of time with him over the past year, telling him about his own experiences of growing up so rapidly, of how he had carved out his place in the world. More than once, Typhoon had stared hard at him and said that he had the qualities of leadership in him.

Daniel sighed. He wished he could be the leader the Brotherhood needed right now. But he couldn't, not when they didn't trust him, and he had no experience in the matter.

He heard footsteps, and Blizzard's voice greeted his nieces and sister-in-law. Daniel pulled a blanket over himself, wishing he had an answer for this situation.

"May I come in?" Blizzard asked.

Daniel rolled over to see Roxy nodding toward the former sheriff. He narrowed his eyes, rolling back to his feet. Blizzard responded with a steady look for a long moment before he looped his thumbs into his belt.

"I understand why," he said, keeping his voice low. Not that it mattered. Everyone in the room was a shifter and would be able to hear what he was saying. "And you did a good thing, saving that girl. You shouldn't have done it, or at least not brought her here, but it was a good thing. But going after Apep now? Suicide. We have our mates and our children to think about, we can't leave them defenseless. Your father, as much as he would love to tear out Apep's throat, knows that, too. He won't let you go."

“What you are forgetting is I’m not a child,” Daniel replied bluntly. “This can’t be solved by wishing it away.”

Blizzard shook his head. “Once you have a plan to take out Apep, the rest of us will listen. But you can’t win by stating what we all know. You need more than to say he has to die, Storm. Otherwise, it’s just us that will die.”

Daniel’s wolf snarled at that, but he nodded. It was true, after all. “I have made the first step in doing just that. Why do you think I brought Gracie here? Even if we don’t know what he wants from her, we know he wants her. And we can use that. We can use *her*.”

Chapter Four

Gracie

How did she get into this situation?

Gracie clutched her purse tightly to her chest, trying not to fidget and look around anxiously. The bank bustled with people. If it wasn't for the constant air of fear and people trying harder than usual to avoid one another's gazes, she would have almost thought it was back before the vampires attacked. Life as usual. Going to the bank, people in a hurry. Everyone involved in their own lives.

Except rather than going to the bank to withdraw money from her account, she was here to rob it. Gracie's head spun as she snuck a glance over her shoulder, to where the hard-eyed woman, only calling herself Shadow, stood with a fake baby in a stroller. Shadow wasn't looking at her, instead fussing with the blanket around her fake baby. Her nervous, jerky movements were perfect for a mother taking her infant out when vampires were running amok, but they weren't helpful in settling Gracie's nerves. Though she knew Shadow was acting, seeing her nervous like that only made Gracie's stomach turn in more knots.

I'm going to be sick.

She sucked in a deep breath to try to steady herself as she advanced in the bank lineup. She was next up for a teller. She fished about in her purse, looking for the note that Daniel had given her, to give to whoever she ended up with. She was weaponless, but many of the shifters were in the bank as well, and they were not weaponless.

She closed her eyes briefly as she remembered Daniel's parting words. *"We need to make sure that Apep knows we have you. He won't come after you himself, he prefers to let others exert themselves, but with any luck, there will be vampires there. And when we can capture one, and finally find out what Apep's plans are…*

So not only was she robbing a bank… but she was also bait in a trap. Either vampires would attack and they'd get one of them, or else vampires wouldn't attack and they'd rob the bank. They needed the funds to continue fighting the vampires, apparently, and if this heist turned out to be a vampire trap rather than a fundraising expedition, they'd be robbing another bank later.

Daniel had told her all of this with a blank expression. And like an idiot, she had volunteered herself. Now, she wished she could go back and slap her past self. This was way over her head...

"I can help you here," one of the tellers called, and Gracie started.

Shaking her head (and the rest of her shaking along) she hurried over to the teller. A nervous smile crossed her lips as she gingerly sat down on the chair before the teller. Her voice came out a loud, high-pitched squeak when she spoke. "Hello! How are you?"

The teller stared at her blankly, probably wondering what sort of idiotic question that was. Heat rushed to Gracie's face as she ducked her head. Silently, she slid the paper across the low counter between them, looking everywhere but the teller. The teller took it, stared at the note for a moment, then looked back up at her.

"Is this a fucking joke?" he demanded.

That wasn't what she had expected. Gracie's face went even redder as she shook her head. "Um... no?"

The teller looked at her, back at her note, and snorted. He started to open his mouth when somebody stepped up behind her. Gracie started badly, but relaxed when she saw it was Daniel. He'd dressed in an unassuming plaid shirt and jeans. With his tanned skin and dark eyes, he looked like a rancher or cowboy. Except for the hard glint to his eyes. That was everything that Gracie had heard about the Savage Brotherhood before she knew they were an army of shifters fighting vampires—ruthless, cruel, arrogant.

"I assure you, there is no mistake," he rumbled in his deep, deep voice. "So, run along and do as we say. Nobody has to be hurt. Better to give it to us than vampires, am I right?"

The subtle threat in his tone changed to one of conspiracy, and he actually winked at the teller. The teller sat there, his mouth half open for several moments before it snapped shut and a red flush rose in his face.

A swell of disappointment hit Gracie hard as Daniel nodded for the teller to go off, his smile most definitely flirtatious. Of course, the most gorgeous man she'd ever met would end up being gay. *I don't know that,* she told herself, *he could be bi or pan or not like labels.*

Or he could just be flirting to get the teller to do what he wants... right?

In any case, the middle of a bank robbery was not when she should be thinking about that... Although, the way life was now, she might die at any moment. Why should she waste time thinking about what was proper? Why not just go for what she wanted right away?

A giggle burst from her throat as she imagined Daniel bending her over the teller's counter and taking her right there. Daniel arched a brow at her and she went very red, turning her face away. And at that moment, a voice cried out from behind them.

"Run!"

Gracie turned. She saw a woman hovering in the air—a vampire. Her face was twisted in fear and anger, and then she was coming at them. Daniel's arm wrapped around Gracie's waist.

The next thing she knew, she was shoved beneath the teller's desk on the other side, shielded on three sides. Daniel was thrown back, impacting the glass doors hard, as the vampire woman smashed into him. She landed lightly, her hands lashing out at him while he held his arms up to defend himself. Their strikes were so quick that Gracie couldn't tell who had the upper hand. She crouched lower, eyes wide. Should she do something? If she swung the teller's chair at them, would she hit the vampire or Daniel? Should she try to run?

Screams filled the bank, then snarls and howls. Savage screams, the sound of fighting. Her heart sank. The vampires had come after her... What could Apep want so badly that he'd do all this... just to get her? Her stomach churned. Was it something special about her, or had he just decided on a whim and now refused to be denied?

"Daniel," the vampire woman gasped as she grabbed him by the back of his neck and smashed his head through a glass window. "I'm sorry... I'm so sorry!"

A sob ripped from her throat, even as she kneed him in the stomach and threw him to the floor, her claws slashing across his throat. Blood splashed the floor and Gracie screamed. The vampire turned, tears streaming down her face. Gracie didn't even see her move; the next moment, the vampire had her, a hand wrapped around her throat as she dragged her out from under the counter.

"The master wants you alive and unharmed," the vampire muttered. "If you've made me kill my boy, I'll find a way to tear you apart, I swear I will!"

Her boy? The tears suddenly made sense. Her apologizing to Daniel even as she beat him up. Gracie stared in horror as the vampire tucked her into her arms and leapt over the teller's counter. Her mouth opened, a protest on her lips.

But then something heavy knocked into them from behind. Gracie was thrown from the vampire's arms. She went skidding across the floor as Daniel wrapped his thick arms around the vampire, pinning her elbows to her sides. Blood trickled down his neck, but his face was hard and determined.

Gracie plunged her hand into her purse, searching for anything that could be used as a weapon. Several more vampires came at her, but their paths were blocked by shifters; most were wolves, but Shadow's leopard jumped in and batted vampires right out of the air. A hand grabbed her arm, and she whirled just as a hand clutched around her arm. She lashed out without even looking at who it was.

The vampire howled and recoiled, stumbling back as he clutched at the pen now struck through his eye. Gracie allowed herself one moment to feel sick to her stomach before she remembered the plan; if the vampires came, she was supposed to take cover. Hurricane and Blizzard would get her out.

She dove for the teller's counter again as Daniel's mother threw her head back, her skull connecting with his nose. He didn't release her, but at that moment the biggest wolf Gracie had ever seen rammed into him from behind. The vampire went flying; she was quickly cornered by Twister, Polaris, and Cyclone. The wolf that attacked Daniel went for his neck, but he rolled and turned back, striking the wolf between the eyes.

Gracie hunkered down, her heart in her throat as she pressed herself to the small lip of the teller's counter. Vampires were being torn apart, their pieces scattering the floor, but the shifters were still fighting.

The wolf shifted into a huge man that swung at Daniel. "Weak, useless boy!" he snarled.

Daniel ducked a blow and punched his enemy in the stomach, but it was clear he had pulled back from striking out with his full strength.

"Don't hold back!" the wolf shouted. "I won't!"

Why was a wolf fighting them? Had some of the shifters joined the vampires? Gracie's breath left her lungs as she remembered what Melanie, Thunder's mate, had told her... that their previous leader was half vampire and was now under Apep's control. But if the vampire woman was Daniel's mother, then that meant...

She must have been turned recently.

"I chose you to be my successor for a reason," the wolf, Typhoon, snarled as Daniel barely managed to dance out of his reach again. "If I knew you'd end up soft, dancing around when real work was to be done, I'd have put you down before you were born!"

Daniel snarled and replied for the first time. "You don't mean that."

Typhoon didn't speak, going after him again. Daniel ducked beneath him, elbowing him in the sternum, then shifted into his wolf form; Typhoon shifted as well, and they started tearing into each other. Horror rose in Gracie's throat. Even as she opened her mouth to scream again, more hands wrapped around her arms.

She let out a startled shriek, struggling instinctively. But this time it was Hurricane who had her. He dragged her to her feet and all but flung her onto Blizzard's back. She clung to his thick fur instinctively as Hurricane shifted as well. They tore out of the bank, Tornado flanking them on one side, Shadow on the other.

A protesting cry ripped from her throat as Daniel let out a pained howl from behind them. She started to twist around, but her grip slipped, and she slid half-off Blizzard's back. With a yelp, she pulled herself back on as his loping gait jostled her from side to side. A vampire came after them, but Thunder jumped into the air, jaws latching around its ankle, and dragged it back to the ground.

Gracie buried her face in Blizzard's fur and shook as visions of blood splashed behind her eyelids. What was going to happen next?

Chapter Five

Storm

Daniel spat into the sink, struggling to tape the bandage to his still-bleeding throat. It was a shallow wound, but more than he should have allowed himself to get. They had been expecting Guinevere and Typhoon to be sent with the attack force... so why had he frozen like that? They could have captured her. He could have his mother back right now if only he hadn't...

He closed his eyes briefly as Typhoon's words returned to his mind. There was no telling if it was something Typhoon himself thought or that Apep was forcing him to say. Could Apep control them that deeply? Make them say certain things?

But then, why would Apep care about breaking down his spirits?

There was a knock on the bathroom door, and Daniel growled under his breath. "I'm not done."

The door opened. He whirled to snap at whoever it was but swallowed it when he saw it was Gracie. Her eyes were red with tears, but she seemed to be taking it rather well. Silently, she pointed at the toilet. When he sat, she rearranged the items in the first aid kit and moved to bandage him up. Having made no progress himself, Daniel let her take over.

"You were very brave," she murmured under her breath. "The way you fought..."

"Wasn't enough. I couldn't..."

Gracie was silent as she washed his neck, then patted it dry. When she started to tape the gauze in place, though, she spoke. "You couldn't save your mother?"

Daniel flinched but nodded.

"When was she turned?"

She hadn't figured it out, then? Daniel hesitated. She didn't know that he was half vampire, and he wasn't certain that he wanted her to know. Not right now, at least. After all, she was the only one in the house who didn't give him that look, the one that was wondering when Apep would take him over. Even his own father looked at him like that, and Roxy didn't let him watch his cousins. Not that she said that outright, but she always had some excuse to stay around when he was there.

A bitter smile crossed his face. It wasn't like Gracie wasn't going to find out… "Sometime during the middle ages. It's a little unclear, she lost track of time in the centuries since." Gracie's hands paused, as he knew they would. He met her wide eyes and nodded. "I'm a hybrid. Half shifter. Half vampire."

"You were… born that way?"

"Yeah. One of only two hybrids known."

Gracie's mouth became an 'o', then she sucked in a breath and turned to the injuries on his shoulders. "Okay."

Daniel couldn't help but snort at that. "That's all you have to say?"

“Yeah. I mean, until three months ago, I didn’t even know vampires or shifters existed. So, you’re a hybrid. That’s no weirder than anything else that’s happened. I didn’t know vampires were born, though.”

“Usually they aren’t. Vamps have a venom that drives shifters crazy and turns humans into vampires as well. As I said, I’m a rarity.” He felt his muscles relax at her gentle touch, cleaning and binding his wounds. Her smell curled into his nostrils and he breathed in deeply, savoring her scent. It was clean and fresh. Smelling her in such close quarters, he understood why Apep would want her. It was tantalizing. He swallowed hard as he caught sight of a scratch on her arm. It had been his plan to use her as bait… and it had nearly landed her in Apep's hands again. "I'm sorry," he blurted.

Gracie glanced up in surprise. "For what?"

"You were almost taken. Because of me."

She blinked a couple of times before her face melted into a smile. Something tightened inside of him at that smile. Daniel found himself unable to stop staring at her lips. Wondering what they would taste like. He wasn't some inexperienced virgin, but the feelings of physical desire always took him by surprise. It never happened unless he got to know the person a little better than the first meeting. Usually knowing them for longer than he knew Gracie.

And yet, as she shifted to wrap a bandage around his arm, all he could think about was how soft her breasts looked at that moment. He wanted to reach out and touch them. Wanted to press her against the door and lift her legs around his waist.

"I wasn't taken because of you." Gracie let out a shuddering breath. "Apep would have killed me or worse already if you hadn't rescued me… and I haven't thanked you for that yet."

Daniel shrugged and glanced away. "Let's just say it's what I do. Besides, it's not like I was just being nice. I have other reasons."

"Does that mean I can't thank you?"

He looked up at her again. There was a hesitant look on her face as she bent over and brushed her lips against his. It was so unexpected that he just sat there for a moment, staring up at her. Even after she learned he was half vampire, she was kissing him?

Gracie backed up, turning her face away. Her cheeks burned bright red. "Sorry!"

"Uh..." How was he supposed to respond to that? To tell her that he was more than fine with it? That he could use a little more kissing. He started to grin at her, but she turned away and hid her face.

"I knew it. I saw the way you smiled at that teller, I shouldn't have... I'm sorry. It's just me being dumb."

The way he smiled at the teller? How had he smiled? He couldn't remember—he'd been too concentrated on getting the teller away, so he could warn Gracie on the approaching scent of vampires. However he'd smiled, though, there was clearly a misunderstanding happening here. Daniel's smirk widened as he stood and turned Gracie back around to face him.

"However I smiled at the teller has nothing to do with that kiss," he told her, then brushed his mouth to hers.

Gracie let out a soft yip, then melted against him. Her arms wrapped around his neck as she teased his lips open and plunged her tongue into his mouth. Daniel tightened, the pressure building in his pants. He grunted as he pressed her against the door, finding her body against his just as soft and well-shaped as he had known it would be.

The world had gone to hell since Apep returned. Everything was different. They could all be dead by the next morning, so why should he hold himself back from what he wanted? And right now, he wanted her. The bathroom was small, but it was big enough for their purposes, and they'd have more privacy in here than anywhere else. His lip curled back with a snarl as he deepened the kiss, his hands reaching for those large, soft breasts to knead between his fingers.

Gracie moaned, reaching between them to cradle him in his jeans. She massaged him, making him grow even harder and he grunted as she did so. She pulled back a little, their breath mingling as their hands roamed each other's bodies. Daniel soon found that the clothes were getting in the way. He needed to touch her skin, needed the warmth of her against him. He grasped the hem of her shirt and yanked it up to her armpits, then reached behind her to unclasp her bra. Her breasts sprang free of their confines, and he just had to taste them.

He bent, sucking on one nipple while her back arched. Gracie let out a soft gasp, her hands flying to his shoulders. He allowed her to move him back, then when her grip tightened and pulled him closer again, he moved to her other breast, nipping at it lightly as he worked his way back up her chest. Gracie's neck and face were flushed pink, her breathing rapid and her eyes bright. She gave him a small, nervous smile, and he stepped back, putting more space between them.

"You okay?"

"Yeah." Her voice was a squeak as she giggled. "I just haven't ever jumped into something this fast before."

Daniel couldn't help but smile at that. "I haven't, either. Guess it's a first time for both of us."

He winked. Gracie giggled again and put her arms around him once more, more relaxed. He kissed her, loving her taste and the feel of her naked breasts against his bare chest. When had his shirt been unbuttoned? It didn't matter. With one hand, he reached down and opened his jeans first, then did the same with her pants. Gracie pushed her pants down impatiently, putting them all the way to her knees.

"I want to fuck you," Daniel hissed in her ear. "From behind with your legs pinned together."

Gracie let out a shiver and a moan. She sucked her lower lip between her teeth and gazed up at him with heated eyes. "Not my ass."

"No," he agreed and gave her a wink as he pushed his fingers between her legs, seeking out her clit. It was already a swollen little nub, liquid dripping from her. "I'm saving that for at least the third date."

Her eyes widened, and she let out a high-pitched giggle that was almost hysterical. Daniel frowned as he made to step back, but she wouldn't let him. She grabbed his wrist to keep his fingers at her clit and let out a shaky breath.

"That sounds nice," she said breathlessly. "I've always been curious... but it's something I've kind of thought... I couldn't say."

“Then you’ve been with the wrong guys.”

Gracie held her breath for a moment, then slid her fingers up his arm until she could make the jump to him. She took him in her hand and started stroking him lightly. He thickened under her touch. His eyes fell to half-mast as he began to pleasure her again. His fingers were soon slippery with her, the scent driving him crazy.

The others were going to want to use the bathroom sooner or later. They didn't have time to make this as long as he’d have liked. With a growl, Daniel turned her, gently bending her over the sink. Gracie gripped the edges, her breathing even quicker as he pressed against her.

“Are you comfortable?” he asked.

At her nod, he eased himself into her. The fit was tighter than he expected; her thighs pressed so tightly together made it difficult for him to get inside her. She shuddered as he entered, though, squeezing down on him. Daniel stroked her back, feeling her muscles and letting out a sigh when she moaned. She felt so good he could spend the rest of his life inside of her. He closed his eyes as he rocked his hips, loving the sensations that flooded his body as he did.

Gracie moaned again, pressing her forehead to the top of the sink as her wetness increased, making his movements smoother. Soon, he was thrusting into her steadily. Her breasts bounced beneath her, and he gripped her ass with one hand, loving the feel of her skin, while the other reached beneath her to find her clit again. He ran his fingers over it, eliciting a loud cry from Gracie.

From there, it all happened very quickly. Her back arched, her legs trembled, and she clamped down so tight on him that he couldn't move. He could almost feel her fluttering; the increased pressure sent him over the edge. He braced himself against the wall, unwilling to crush her to the sink, and thrust his hips another few times as pleasure burst through him. He emptied into her with a series of grunts, then was still.

Gracie's back twitched as she lay over the sink, moaning and gasping. Daniel gently withdrew from her, then stumbled over to the toilet and sat before pulling her into his lap. Her face was flushed, her hair mussed, and she gave him a smile as she sank into his embrace.

"Thank you," she whispered.

Daniel buried his face into her hair and breathed in her scent. What was she thanking him for, when it was him that ought to be thanking her? He smiled as his arms tightened... he hadn't realized until now how lonely he had been. But while she was here, he didn't have to be lonely anymore.

Chapter Six

Gracie

Gracie blushed at the scrutiny she found herself under, with twelve sets of eyes staring at her. Shadow's oldest girls were watching all the younger children, so that the adults could gather together and discuss what to do with her now. Daniel lounged beside her, seemingly unbothered by the looks that ranged from distrustful to so blank she couldn't read them. She was glad to see some sympathy, but it wasn't enough to hide the looks that clearly wondered if they ought to just kick her out and preserve themselves.

Eventually, Ava spoke. "Did you find anything unusual on your exam?"

The question was not directed at Gracie, but at Mia.

The tiger-shifter doctor shook her head. "She's as ordinary as millions of women all over the planet. Nothing special about her bloodwork that I could find. Of course, I don't have all my resources here. If there is something physically different about her, I'd need more equipment to find out."

Gracie rubbed her hands together and glanced around at them all. "If I knew what Apep wanted from me, I'd tell you."

"We know that," Daniel answered in his deep rumble. He took her hand and squeezed it. The gesture did not go unnoticed, with Roxy, Twister, Polaris, Hurricane, and Cyclone all frowning while the others looked even more blank-faced, except for Ava and Melanie, both of whom grinned. Daniel gave no indication that he noticed the looks they were given, though. Which was just as well, because Gracie had heard quite enough of Twister and Roxy scolding him for sleeping with her already. "Don't worry, we're going to figure this out. Apep's pulling out all the stops to get you back—"

"Or he sent Typhoon and Guinevere to take us out, like he's been doing from the start," Polaris gently chided. "It's not necessarily about Gracie."

Shadow moved up beside her mate, arms crossed tightly over her chest. "Guinevere said Apep wants the girl alive and unharmed. So, he wants her for something... I don't relish the idea of killing an innocent, but—"

Gracie shrank back from her as Daniel leapt to his feet and snarled blackly.

"I'm not saying that we kill her right now," Shadow snapped. "But if it comes to it, we kill her rather than let her fall in Apep's hands. Or would you rather be his prisoner, with whatever he has planned for you?" Shadow glowered at Gracie here, as though daring her to say she'd rather go to Apep than die.

Gracie stared back at her, not about to answer. Of course, she didn't want to be Apep's prisoner! But she didn't want to give Shadow permission to kill her. The leopard shifter seemed like the kind of person who would do hard things and live with the guilt of it, rather than risk even worse things happening. If they'd discussed this before, would she have killed Gracie at the bank, rather than try to rescue her and risk capture?

"We're not killing anybody," Mia spat, her voice harsher and stronger than Gracie had heard it before. She glared at Shadow for a moment before sweeping her gaze over all of them. "So Guinevere said that Apep wanted her alive. The last time I saw Rob—Typhoon—he said that he only put up with Jasper because he liked fucking me. You all know how much he loves our son. Apep can make them say things they don't mean. For all we know, Apep wants her dead and had Guinevere say that to get us to kill her for him."

Everyone was silent for a moment. Daniel returned to sit beside Gracie, taking her hand once more. Somehow it felt even more intimate than when they had slept together. Not that there was any sleeping involved… They'd only had the one round before Twister came pounding on the door and started to scold Daniel for getting involved with her when they knew nothing about her.

Twister scowled at her now, but there was clear worry in his eyes. He was rather overprotective, Gracie thought, considering that he couldn't be that much older than Daniel.

"Speaking of Typhoon." It was Tornado who spoke this time. His jaw clenched as his gaze swept to Mia, and then Twister. "We've danced around the subject long enough. How long did you know that he was half vampire?"

Mia's eyes hardened as she glared back at Tornado. "Since he told me," she replied bluntly. "And he told Twister because Guinevere was pregnant, and they needed to know what to expect with Storm."

Gracie straightened. What? Twister was Guinevere's mate? Her brow furrowed as her gaze flashed between them. But he was far too young to be Daniel's father… but what Mia had just said made it sound like he was… *Shifters must age differently than humans,* she thought. *Twister must be older than he looks.*

She was going to have to ask Daniel about this…

"You've had three months to bitch about this and quite frankly I'm tired of listening to you."

Tornado exposed a canine. "It's just that if I'd known he was half bloodsucker, I never would have followed him. And I can't help but wonder why you would fuck him still... not that Twister's motives are any surprise, what with fucking a bloodsucking queen himself."

Gracie flinched back as Mia leapt at Twister, black and orange fur sprouting from her body. Twister let out a snarl and was held back by Cyclone and Polaris. To Gracie's surprise, it was Daniel that grabbed Mia and held her sharp claws back from slicing open Tornado's face as Shadow prepared to spring, Blizzard beside her. Roxy and Hurricane both placed themselves in front of Melanie and Ava, shielding them as they both shied back.

"That's enough," Daniel snapped, his hold tight around Mia. "Who are you helping with that Tornado?"

"I don't think a half vamp has any right to—"

"WHO ARE YOU HELPING?" Daniel roared, loud enough to make Gracie flinch again. Her heart started pounding faster and she jumped to her feet, ready to run if she needed to. Her hands were cold, her entire focus on Daniel and Tornado now; he still held onto Mia, but it was almost as though he was holding himself back by holding her.

Tornado's nostrils flared, and he opened his mouth, but Ava skirted around the room and put a hand on his chest. "Apep."

Tornado gave her a startled glance. "What?"

"When you talk like that, you're only helping Apep. Typhoon isn't the one who summoned him back. And when you go around calling him a bloodsucker and saying such crude and cruel things to your allies about people they love…" Ava put her hands on her hips and glowered at her mate. "Can you blame him for not telling you? Now I want you to apologize or you're sleeping on the couch tonight."

Tornado had the decency to look ashamed. He squeezed the back of his neck before glancing up at Daniel, Twister, and Mia. "I'm sorry. I didn't mean it. My mouth runs off with my head sometimes."

Daniel relaxed and released Mia. He nodded. "We know that. But can we all just try not to be so hot-headed? We can't allow ourselves to be torn apart, not when we're all we have against Apep. We can't rely on anybody else. We need to get on the same page here."

Nobody responded to that, although Gracie thought it had been a rather good little speech. She stepped up next to Daniel and blurted out the only thing she could think to say. “He’s still afraid of you, you know. You’re on the news all the time. The Savage Brotherhood, talking about what horrible things you do and how you’re out to enslave humanity and how he’s trying to protect us from you guys. He wouldn’t be making such an effort to demonize you if he wasn’t afraid.”

Shadow smirked at that, though it was short lived. “Thank God it’s not us that are scared, then.”

Thunder, who until now had been silent and still, stood and nodded in Daniel’s direction. “The kid is right. We are too divided. What we need is a real leader here. The more we vie for the position, the most splintered we become. The problem is that we all think we ought to be the alpha, and our mates will naturally vote for us."

"I don't think I should be alpha," Cyclone said mildly.

Thunder rolled his eyes but smirked. "Right. So, we should all put the name of the one we think will be the best alpha in a hat. Winner becomes alpha and we follow his lead."

"So sure it'd be a him?" Melanie interrupted.

Thunder opened his mouth, but he'd already lost them. Gracie's eyebrows rose as they fell to squabbling about semantics and how fair a vote actually would be, whether they should include the children or at least the teens. She leaned back, shaking her head. It was obvious that they did need a leader... and she knew who she thought would be best at it. But would she even be allowed a vote?

Shadow was the first to leave the room, with a snarl over her shoulder while Blizzard followed after her, glaring at the rest of them as though they might attack. "If we don't keep our heads, we're going to lose them."

Snorts answered the statement. Gracie took Daniel's hand, seeing the tension in his neck and shoulders, and gently tugged him from the room. It was so crowded in there she could hardly breathe, and the tension wasn't helping it any. She and Daniel headed up for the attic, the only open space where they could get any sort of privacy. It was far too cold to think about doing anything besides just sitting and talking though, and even that couldn't last long.

"I think I'm going to sleep up here tonight," Daniel grumbled as he stretched out on the thick two-by-fours. "Maybe that way I can get some actual rest. It won't be too cold if I'm in my wolf form."

"If you roll over, you'll fall through the ceiling."

"I can find some plywood to throw down, give myself a bit of a bed."

Gracie smiled briefly, but it didn't last long. "Thunder's right. There needs to be a clear leader here."

Daniel shrugged, staring at the underside of the roof. Bits of snow drifted in through it. A couple of flakes landed on her nose and Gracie scrubbed them off. She wrapped her arms around herself as she considered him.

"Do you think—"

"We've tried to decide on a leader before," Daniel interrupted. "We even voted. Eliminating those with the fewest votes and revolting. It ended up in a tie and nobody even listened to the person they voted for. We shifters aren't built like that. We need someone to take leadership, to dominate the others. The problem is that we just have too many strong alphas here already."

His tone made it clear that the discussion was over. Gracie bit her tongue, wanting to press the issue but knowing it would do no good. Instead, she turned her mind to something else.

"What do we know about Apep?"

Daniel gave her a surprised look.

"He can control the vampires," something she didn't know until she came here, "and he's an Egyptian god. But what else?"

He didn't answer.

"I take that to mean nothing?"

He shrugged, a blush creeping into his cheeks.

Gracie sighed. "Well, at least that's something I can do. If you can get me internet access, I'll start researching. Maybe we can find out something that will be useful. And I won't have to sit around listening to people talking about the benefits of killing me outright."

Daniel rolled to a sitting position. He reached for her hand and clasped it tightly. “No one is going to kill you. I promise.”

Chapter Seven

Storm

They needed more money. Since none of them could go out and get a job without inviting Apep's forces down on their heads while flipping burgers, robbery was the only option. And it was one that they had all taken part in before Apep's attack—well, Daniel had had everything provided for him, but he had been planning on joining the Brotherhood before Apep's attack—and so it was an easy choice for them.

This time, they needed it to go smoothly. So, they had scoured all the banks, picked one that would be the least likely for Apep to be watching, and made a plan to rob it. It wasn't easy, since everybody had their own ideas on how to go about it. One thing that all of them, Daniel included, agreed on, however, was that Gracie was not coming with them.

The morning that they were going to head out, he headed up to the attic. He'd gotten some boards and nails to patch it up, and a heater plus extension cord made it bearable to be in. So far it was his and Gracie's private place, but it was only a matter of time before the others expanded into the territory as well.

He found her there, sitting close to the heater, bundled up in a thick coat as she poured over the books he'd managed to steal from Guinevere's library, before he was chased off when Apep first made his appearance. Beside her was a stack of books he'd stolen from a library. She was a dedicated researcher, it seemed, and a smile tugged up his lips.

"Hey."

She jumped, then blushed as she smiled up at him. "Didn't hear you come up."

"I was quiet." He winked at her. "So, we're headed off here soon. Anything you need before we leave?"

Gracie placed her bookmark and crooked her finger toward him. "A goodbye kiss?"

A grin crossed his face as he bent over her. The hot air from the space heater brushed over his skin as he laid her down on the platform he'd built, pressing himself against her. The wood was cold, the air chilly, but her warm body against his made it worth it.

"When are you leaving?" she moaned once their lips parted.

"About an hour."

Gracie wrapped her arms around his neck and toyed with the hairs on the back of his neck. "That's long enough."

Daniel's eyes darkened with lust as he considered her. Yes, it was long enough for what he wanted. To get her sopping wet, to find his place inside of her and mark her as his own. It was the situation, he knew, that was drawing them so close together. Only Mia and Andy were without their mates, and it got lonely watching the others cuddling next to each other. It wasn't like Gracie was his forever girl, but when they could be killed at any time... why not wrap up in each other and take what comfort they could?

Several layers were between them, but Daniel made quick work of them. He draped one of the blankets over their hips to give a bit more warmth, and from there it was quick. He made sure she finished before him, and then they lay with their arms around each other. It had only taken half an hour, and they could probably have another round, but Daniel found himself satisfied at the moment—he just wanted to hold her.

"Can I ask you something?" her lips were plump and swollen from their kisses as she licked them.

Daniel propped himself on an elbow and nodded.

"You're Andy's son?"

Hadn't she known that already? They didn't make it a secret. He arched a brow and nodded again.

"Oh." Gracie glanced away. "I thought he was your brother. You two look so close age."

A ball of dread started to build in his stomach. She was going to ask. And he was going to have to give her the answer. How was she going to react to learning that he was, chronologically, less than two years old? It didn't change the fact that he was physically and mentally just as old as his father... but that was sometimes difficult for people to understand when they knew his age.

Luckily, she didn't go there—not right away, at least.

"So, Typhoon was the former alpha of the Brotherhood? And since he's half vampire, Apep was able to take control of him?"

"Yeah."

Gracie hesitated a moment. "He was the one that attacked you at the bank."

"Yeah." Why was she asking about Typhoon?

"Why was he controlled… but not you?"

Daniel let out a heavy sigh. "I don't know. I wish I did. Maybe then we'd be able to figure out a way to end Apep's control over all of them. But the truth is… I don't know if I am immune. Or if Apep is just waiting for the right moment to take me, too. Or maybe I'm just not strong enough to be of use to him."

Gracie frowned. "Maybe it has something to do with the amount of vampire in you. I mean, it's genetics, right? Maybe you have more shifter or something like that."

Daniel frowned. He hadn't thought of that before... Perhaps his mother had drunk more shifter blood and was, therefore, more human when he was conceived than Typhoon's father... "My mother is a vampire; his father is a vampire. You think it could be that? Like the difference between a Liger and a Tigon? We're different types of hybrids?"

"Maybe."

Well, they couldn't exactly compare DNA to find out. He rolled over and pulled up his pants, still frowning. "Typhoon always suppressed his vampire side, too. But I grew up with vampires... for the longest time, I couldn't shift into a wolf. I thought that maybe I didn't have enough shifter in me. I wondered if maybe... maybe I embraced the vampire side of me enough that it's not overpowering the shifter side of me? I don't know if that makes sense."

Gracie wrapped the blanket around herself and frowned. "It does... maybe him suppressing that side of him meant that he didn't have control of it and that it left him vulnerable?"

"Yeah. Something like that." Daniel nodded, relieved that she understood. It was also a relief to be able to talk about these things with someone. His family and Mia remained the only ones who were accepting of his half vampire status, but even they feared he might suddenly be taken over. There was just so much pain with the whole situation, too. It was just... messy. "If we could figure it out, though… maybe there is something physically different about me. I haven't had even the urge to obey Apep, not even when he first appeared."

"Maybe it's the hybrid thing." Gracie frowned as she sat up and reached for a book. "I'm not a geneticist, but maybe there's something in legends… Uh… Sekhmet was a shifter! I think. If she was real like Apep, then maybe she was a hybrid? The legends say she fell to bloodlust and was only stopped by beer that looked like blood."

Daniel chuckled under his breath as he watched her. The determined furrow in her brow made him grin. "So, what you're saying is we need to get Typhoon drunk?"

"It couldn't hurt."

"Well, I'll get right on that."

“Typhoon said he was training you to take over after him.” Gracie shut the book again and gave him a hard look. “So why aren’t you their leader? You say that someone needs to take leadership... what’s holding you back?”

Daniel’s brow arched. He hadn’t been expected that question, certainly not with the level of accusation in her voice. He wasn’t certain how to respond at first, but her expression made it clear she wasn’t going to back down until she had an answer. He chewed his cheek then shrugged.

“Guess I don’t want to cause more troubles. They don’t trust me. I’m half bloodsucker, as Tornado said. I could turn on them at any moment.”

“Yet you were the one who was able to get him to back down.”

Daniel rolled his eyes. "Ava did that."

"But you followed it through," Gracie insisted. Her eyes flashed as she shoved her hands into her sleeves for warmth. "You have the strength to be the leader, and I think you're right. Whatever strategies you're using aren't working. Apep is getting stronger and those who oppose him are getting weaker. So. Why not you?"

"They think if me as a kid."

Gracie's brow furrowed. "But they all look the same age as you! So what, do shifters age slower once they hit their twenties or something?"

Daniel shook his head. That dread was returning, but he attempted to keep his voice casual and his expression smooth. "No. Well, shifters live longer than humans, but it's more along the lines of not deteriorating as fast in old age. No, the reason they think of me as a kid is because vampire-shifter hybrids age more rapidly than humans or shifters."

Gracie's brow puckered.

"You have to understand," he said slowly, watching her for the strike of realization, "that when I was born, I already had the mental capacity of a ten-year-old. I've never really been a child, and I am mentally and emotionally as old as I look physically."

Understanding started to dawn, and her eyes widened.

"I was born less than two years ago. I matured to adulthood by my first birthday. Then... well, we don't really know the details. Typhoon had similar development as me. He's aged normally from that time."

Gracie paled. She drew back from him, a look of horror coming over her face.

"I am not a child," Daniel was quick to assure her. He didn't want to lose her now... not when she felt like his anchor in the waves of doubt that ate at him. "I might lack a bit in life experiences, but I am as much an adult as you are."

Gracie nodded, looking sick. His heart sank, and he withdrew a little. She wasn't going to accept it. Like the others, she was going to ignore the fact that he wasn't a child in a man's body and think only of his age. His wolf nudged his chest, trying to get him to embrace her, to prove with his body that he was no child, but he shoved it back angrily. He didn't need that right now.

"You can ask the others," he said, glancing away. "Since I understand why you wouldn't believe me. But Gracie... You have been with us for a few weeks. Have I ever acted like a child?"

She didn't respond. Not that he expected her to. Andy called from below and Daniel stood, making sure he was covered before he headed out of the attic. He glanced back just before Gracie was out of sight to find her holding her head in her hands. A pang hit his stomach, but he dropped out and headed to join with his father and the others.

If she couldn't accept it, then he'd have to step back. That was the adult thing to do. Besides, with a god risen from the dead and wanting to kill them all, he didn't have the time to be distracted by a girl. If circumstances were different... but he couldn't take the time right now. And it hurt, yeah, but he'd get over it.

He'd get over her.

Chapter Eight

Gracie

Children in the other room were crying and she could hear Melanie trying to soothe them. In the tiny kitchen, hardly big enough for the table shoved into the corner, the older kids peeled vegetables, helping prepare the stew for when the others returned home. Ava had gone out some time ago and returned with a handful of rabbits, which she had skinned expertly and was now chopping into bits for the stew.

Gracie brushed some of the hair from her eyes as she finished pealing the last potato. It had been hours since the others left, and her stomach was tied into such knots that the lack of conversation was stifling. She wanted to say something, anything, to get her mind off what was happening out there, but her mind was an utter blank.

"We're done," the oldest girl, Artemis, declared as she pushed herself to her feet. Her sisters, Freya and Sekhmet, followed suit. "We're going up to the attic to read now."

Gracie grimaced. She knew why they would want to get away from all the noise, but she still thought of the attic as her and Daniel's space. She didn't want to share it. Still, she nodded at them, letting them go. It wasn't like it would take her long to chop up the vegetables.

The girls streamed from the room and Ava tipped her cut-up meat into the stew pot. She let out a heavy sigh, heavier than Gracie had heard, and rinsed off the cutting board before washing her hands. Once she was done with that, Ava joined Gracie at the table, cutting the potatoes.

"It's like this," she said unexpectedly. "The waiting. When you're mated to one of the Savage Brotherhood, it's your life. Always waiting for them to return, always fearing something will go wrong. I can't tell you how many times I've waited up all night for Jackson, wondering what I would tell our children if he never returned."

Gracie flinched. "That sounds... awful."

"It is. But he's always come home."

"What about before the vampires? I mean... the Savage Brotherhood is a well-known gang. I've heard some pretty terrible things about them."

Ava's expression darkened as her shoulders hunched. "That was the hardest part to accept. But they have always, first and foremost, been an army against the vamps. The criminal activity was just a way to fund it. You can't exactly hold down a full-time job when you can be called to go fight the undead at any moment, after all."

"That's the thing that almost pulled me and Zane apart before we were even mates," Melanie spoke from the doorway and Gracie jumped. She came in, holding a five-month-old baby. "I was terrified of the Brotherhood. Thought they were nothing but no-good gangsters. Even after I learned the truth, it was difficult for me to accept. But I knew that Zane had a deeper mission. He would sacrifice so much of his personal happiness to stop vampires from taking over…"

She trailed off, and Gracie knew what she was thinking. Vampires had taken over anyway.

Melanie shook her head and sighed. "I'm just glad his mother passed away peacefully before all of this happened. She had a good, full life and got to meet her grandchildren, and they got to meet her. I don't think she would have survived Apep's return."

Ava reached out and squeezed Melanie's hand. "Have you heard about your father?"

"Safe, for now." Catching Gracie's confused look, Melanie explained. "My father has been sick for a long time. We couldn't risk dragging him all over the place. But he's not a shifter, so the vampires don't seem to care about him. Apep has not gone after non-shifter family."

Gracie shivered at the thought. She almost preferred the silence to this.

Melanie sighed. "I'm sorry if this makes you more anxious. We try not to talk like this around the children or Mia. I have to say, though, you seem to be doing quite well. Considering everything that's been thrown at you, you're holding up well."

"Thanks. I feel like I could fly apart at any second."

Ava paused a moment, then a sly smile crossed her face. "Bet Storm helps with that."

Gracie's stomach twisted tighter. She dropped her knife and leaned her elbows against the table. “Is he really only two years old?”

She glanced up to see the other women glance at each other. Their expressions sobered; Melanie shrugged as she passed the baby to Gracie and took over chopping vegetables.

“He’s the first vampire-shifter hybrid I heard of,” Ava said. “I mean, I know that Typhoon is now, but I have no idea how old he is. From what I recall, he only showed up in the Brotherhood about fifteen years ago. Storm has never acted like a kid. The first time we met, he started talking about the allegory of Plato’s Cave.”

That wasn’t helpful. Gracie shifted the baby to be more comfortable and sighed. “It’s just... Yeah, he looks grown up and he acts it, but if he’s really only lived two years... I mean, he doesn't have the experiences, right? No matter how mature he might be, it's the experience..."

Melanie looked thoughtful as she nodded. "I get what you mean. I think it's something you should probably discuss with him. I know that you're not the first woman he's had a relationship with. I don't know. You could talk with Mia about Typhoon."

Gracie thought about the tiger shifter's sad face and the way she always seemed to be on the verge of tears. Bringing up her lost mate wasn't what Gracie wanted to do at all. She nodded doubtfully anyway, wanting to get off this topic. She cast her mind about, but no other topic came, really. Except for getting back to the vampires. Melanie said her father was still out there. As she glanced between the two of them, though, she wondered why it was just them, their mates and their children. Surely out of all of them, there had to be brothers, sisters, parents?

"Have... have you lost anybody?" she asked hesitantly. "To the vampires."

Ava shivered. "Not anybody that I was close to. We've lost plenty of the Brotherhood but—"

"I meant... family. Friends."

Melanie shook her head. "No. Not yet, at least. It's something we can be thankful for at least."

"And you?" Ava's voice was so soft Gracie almost missed it. "Have you lost anyone?"

Gracie sighed. "No. I never really had anybody to lose. I've lived a pretty isolated life... and now I'm glad I did. I can't imagine how it would be, waiting to hear if the vampires were going after someone I cared about. But my parents never really had anything to do with me, and they both died when I was in my teens. My grandparents took me in, and they passed several years ago. Don't really have friends..."

Melanie opened her mouth, but before she could speak there was a shriek from somewhere in the house. The word wasn't clear, but the tone of fear was. *Vampires*.

All three women leapt to their feet. Melanie snatched the baby back from Gracie, and they all dashed from the kitchen. Snarls filled the air as Gracie ran for the emergency packs; she was to gather the supplies while Melanie and Roxy gathered the children. Mia and Ava both shifted into their feline forms and attacked the vampires as they streamed into the safehouse. Artemis and Sekhmet joined them while Freya raced to help Gracie.

Gracie grabbed the packs, putting herself between Freya and the oncoming vampires. Blood tainted the air and there was a thick smell of rotting fruit that made her gag. Gracie headed for the van, her heart thumping as the little ones raced ahead of Melanie, the baby still clutched in her arms. They got them into the van parked in the garage, and then Gracie remembered—the books. They needed the books! If they had any chance at finding what Apep actually was…

"Go," she told Melanie urgently, struggling to buckle in the little ones. There wasn't any more time; the vicious snarls were growing more desperate. Gracie's heart thumped hard. "I can take one of the bikes. Go!"

"Gracie, we stick to the plan—" Roxy started.

"Just go!"

Gracie slammed the door and rushed back into the house. She didn't turn back as Melanie stomped on the gas and peeled out of the garage, smashing the door open as she did so. She leaned on the horn; the signal to the other women it was time to split. There was a yowl and a scream of pain. Gracie rushed to the attic, hoping desperately that the vampires would try to chase after the feline shifters.

She got to the attic and shoved the books into the pack when she heard footsteps below. Her heart slammed against her chest, and then the smell of smoke started to curl into her nostrils. She looked around rapidly, trying to find some escape route—there was none except to go straight down.

Holding her breath, she slipped down the ladder. The sound of flickering flames reached her ears, and she dashed across the hall, headed for the bikes...

A hand snaked out of nowhere and grabbed her arm. She turned, gasping, and something heavy hit her head. Everything went black.

***

The blackness greeted her when she awoke. A chill seeped into her bones as pain pounded through her head. Nausea swirled in her stomach, and she took a moment to try to orient herself before she moved. Not that it did much good—as soon as she sat up, a grating noise pieced her skull and lights stabbed her eyes.

A vampire—the vampire she had seen at the bank, Daniel's mother—entered the room and lifted Gracie to her feet.

"Easy," she murmured as Gracie tried to rip herself away. "I'm sorry."

Gracie's stomach churned with bile as she tried vainly to free herself from the vampire's strong grip. "What's going to happen to me?" she gasped.

Guinevere didn't answer. She brought Gracie out of the room and down a long, cold hallway. Within moments, they were standing in a lavishly decorated office. Typhoon knelt by the desk, an expression of hatred on his face. A collar was latched around his throat, a bowl of water and another with some raw meat in it beside the first. Gracie's stomach churned harder as his eyes widened and a look of devastation crossed his face.

"Ah, and here she is."

The smooth voice from behind her made her shudder. Fighting the urge to be sick, Gracie turned to see Apep smiling down at her. He sauntered forward to cup her face with one heavily jeweled hand. "Finally, we get to meet. I have been looking for you for a long time, Gracie Underhill. You are a hard woman to find."

Guinevere released her and stepped back, hands clasped before her while her chin fell to her chest. Gracie bunched her hands. If she had a stake, she could stab Apep in the heart! If only she had some sort of weapon...

Apep sighed happily as he released her. He stepped back, his gaze traveling down her form before he nodded. "You look stronger than the others... Let's hope you survive, shall we?"

Dread swept through her. Apep laughed and Gracie began to tremble. What was he going to do to her?

Chapter Nine

Storm

They saw the smoke rising from the safehouse before they arrived; Daniel's stomach clenched, the victory of their successful bank robbery swept from his mind. Tornado and Thunder both sped up, leaning over the handles of their bikes; Daniel put on a burst of speed and got ahead of them, turning his bike sideways to cut them off.

"We stick to the plan," he snarled. "We get to the beta site, meet up with them there. It won't do anybody any good if we end up dead here."

Thunder growled at him, but Daniel snarled right back. His heart slammed into his ribs, and he wanted to rush to the burning safehouse as much as any of the others—he could see the fear on Shadow's face, the paleness of Hurricane's skin. His stomach twisted in knots as he thought of his aunt, his cousins, of the children they left there... and of Gracie.

But he took a deep breath and glowered at the others, forcing himself to think instead about what would happen if they went to the safe house and were ambushed by vampires as their mates and children were at the beta site.

"We have to stick to the plan," he reminded them and wheeled his bike around.

The bags of money strapped to the back seemed to weigh him down; luckily, Andy, Stewart, and Polaris turned with him; after a moment, Josef did as well. And then Thunder reluctantly came, followed by Tornado.

Shadow was the last to obey, her expression one of terror now; that more than anything made Daniel feel like he was about to be sick. He'd never seen Shadow, of all people, look so afraid.

They drove quickly toward the beta site. It was just an open area in the woods, from way back before the Savage Brotherhood was formed; it had been charmed against vampires, but there was no protection from the elements there, and with the thick brush it would be difficult to see the vampires coming after them.

Relief washed over Daniel as they pulled up to the sight to find the van and bikes they'd left behind there. The others rushed forward, embracing mates and children. Andy stopped beside Daniel and gripped his arm; Daniel knew instantly why.

Gracie was nowhere in sight, and he couldn't smell her.

"Daniel—" his father started.

Daniel tore away from him and raced for Roxy. "Where's Gracie?"

His aunt gave him a look of deep pity. "She told us to leave; she was going back, I don't know what for. We couldn't wait, we had the children."

His throat was thick as he whispered. "Where is she?"

Melanie stepped up beside Roxy and put a hand on her shoulder. "We had to leave her."

"Typhoon took her," Mia interrupted. Her voice was emotionless, as though she was hurting too deeply to feel anymore. Tears welled in her eyes even as she wiped them away. "I saw him as I was leaving. He had her slung over his back."

Daniel slumped over. He pressed his hands to his knees, his mind whirling as he tried to accept this news. Images flashed through his mind of Gracie when he first saw her in that hospital robe, the terror on her face. The look in her eyes when he had brought her to the safehouse. The smile on her lips when she kissed him. The way her eyes rolled and her back arched when he finished into her.

Then he thought of her in Apep's hands. Of her skin marble-white, her eyes dull and lifeless. His wolf threw back its head and howled. A snarl burst from his throat; the children scattered, their parents tensed, and the men stepped in front of their mates—even Stewart and Josef. Daniel didn't waste any time feeling bad that even his uncles felt like they had to defend his aunts.

His head snapped up and he focused on Shadow. “You’re coming with me.”

Blizzard snarled, tensing. “She’s not—”

“Cunningham,” Shadow cut across him, giving him the stink eye.

Blizzard hesitated a moment before he stepped aside and gestured at her. Which was just as well; they might be mates, but Daniel knew that Shadow didn’t let anybody tell her what she could and could not do—unless they were acting like an alpha. Daniel drew himself up. His conversation with Gracie came back to him, and he wanted to growl again—this time in anger at himself. He hadn’t thought it a good idea to stay at the safe house for so long, but the others all said it would be too hard on the children to keep running. He should have just insisted that they leave!

His wolf growled, but he pulled it back and centered on the present. "Shadow, you're going to help me track down where he took her."

"Whoa." Tornado held up a hand. "You can't do that. One girl isn't worth that risk, even if you have been sleeping with her."

Shadow didn't speak.

Daniel took a moment to calm himself down before he spoke again. "We don't know what Apep wants from her."

"Daniel." Andy strode forward and gripped his shoulder. "Listen. I know that you've grown close to her. I know that this must be tearing you up. But they were backing off until we got her again. We can't risk having her around. I'm sorry," he said, his voice hardening as Daniel snarled. "I don't like it any more than you do. But we have to think about what's best for everyone."

No. He didn't want to think about what was best for everyone. He wanted to get Gracie back. Had to get her back. He couldn't leave her out there, God knew what was happening to her. Apep could be doing any sort of depraved thing to her, and if he just abandoned her to that fate? Then what use was he? He glared at his father then turned the glare on everyone else.

The children were hiding behind their parents, staring at him in terror. Daniel almost growled, wondering what sort of things they had been told to make them react like this. Even his cousins! But then he felt the fierce scowl on his face and knew it was him that they were fearing, not words their parents had said.

He closed his eyes and turned away. His father was right—he needed to think about everyone. That was what a leader did, after all. If he only thought about himself and his wants, he was as useless as if he left Gracie to be Apep's pray.

So what should he do?

A deep breath stabilized him, and he turned back. Everyone stared at him, waiting, expectant, a few hostile glances. Looks he had seen directed at Typhoon multiple times. Daniel drew himself up, striding forward to glance around the area.

"Get out into the woods and gather branches and brush to make shelters. Every family has their own lean-to," he ordered. "No fires. We'll use the camping stove to cook. Now." He turned to Shadow. "You and I are going to track down where Typhoon took Gracie. We can't keep running around like chickens with their heads cut off."

Both Blizzard and Tornado started to protest, but Shadow nodded. "What are we waiting for?"

They headed for the bikes, even as there were murmurs and grumbles behind them. Andy gave him a look that was half confused, half worried but Daniel ignored it. If he wanted to stop them thinking of him as a kid, then he had to force them to see he wasn't a kid. And he was going to get Gracie back. That was non-negotiable.

Shadow was one of the best trackers Daniel knew. But after they found a backpack full of the books Gracie had been going through, they lost the trail. No amount of back-tracking could pick it up again. It wasn't all in vain, though. When they returned to the safehouse, they found a vampire poking through the ruins.

They quickly jumped him, tied him up and dragged him into the forest. They weren't going to take him to where their new camp was, of course, but there might be something that they could learn from him.

Daniel's knuckles were sore and bruised by the time the vampire spoke, spitting blood from his mouth. “The girl is unique. Apep has traced her lineage back further than time itself.”

Shadow sat nearby, sharpening her claws and looking profoundly bored. At the vampire’s declaration, she snorted and rolled her eyes. “Before time, huh? And what is so special about her lineage?”

“She is a true descendant from the first shifter, from Ra himself.”

Daniel’s eyes narrowed. First shifter? Ra? He was tempted to punch the vampire another few times and tell him not to babble nonsense, but he held himself back. If Apep was the first vampire, then it did make some sort of sense that Ra, Apep’s enemy, would be the first shifter... they had been enemies for as long as Daniel knew, after all.

"Supposing that's true," he said slowly, "what do you mean by true descendant? She's not a shifter."

The vampire turned and sneered at him. "Humans can be turned into shifters with your rituals and a bite just as a human can become a vampire. And isn't it true that when a child is born to two shifters, that child is not always a shifter themselves?"

It was true. Daniel's frown deepened. "So, what you're saying is that Gracie is a *direct* descendant of the first shifter... who is Ra? Is Apep trying to resurrect him or something?"

The vampire stared at him as though that was the stupidest thing he had ever heard.

Daniel nodded at Shadow, who marched over and sliced the vampire across the face. "It's time you and I started talking. This is how I do things. I ask you a question, you answer. I think you're lying, I cut you. I don't like your answer, I cut you. Now. What does Apep want with the girl?"

The vampire grunted. "What do I care about your threats? I am a vampire. Pain is nothing to me."

"That's because you haven't felt pain. Not since you became a vampire." Shadow smiled chillingly. "But you know what happens when a vampire drinks shifter blood, right? They become human again, at least for a time. And then all those dead nerves in your body? They'll come *screaming* back to life."

All arrogance drained from of the vampire's face as Daniel brought his own wrist to his mouth, growing out his fangs to sink into his flesh; as a half vampire, he was immune to vampire venom.

The vampire lasted only a few swallows of Daniel's blood before he was begging for them to stop.

"We don't know what he wants from her," he gasped, his pale cheeks flushed with human color. "I don't know. All he'd say was she was a descendant of Ra. The others... he would drink their blood and do something. I don't know what, I never saw, I only heard rumors. But he was angry when they died. He's hoping she's the one that will live."

Daniel glowered at the vampire but took a step back and glanced at Shadow. She nodded, showing she believed the vamp. Daniel turned away and cursed.

What did Apep want? And how could they stop him?

Shadow stepped up beside him. "What now?"

He closed his eyes and inhaled deeply. "We find where Apep took her. And then we get her back. In the meantime," he grabbed the bag of books. "We're going to find out his weaknesses. And we're going to make a plan to kill him."

Chapter Ten

Gracie

The ice-cold grips on her arms were like iron. Though Gracie kicked and screamed and cried, they didn't seem to take any notice. Tears streaked her face as she was dragged out of the pitch-dark underground. She had thought it would be a relief to be above ground again, to breathe fresh air and have natural light. But that was before she was dragged from her cell, changed into a revealing, low-cut gown and then dragged out to face Apep.

The light of a full moon bathed the land in a silvery light. It was so bright that she could see everything in vivid detail. Apep stood in the center of some design carved into the rock, one with curving lines and strange symbols around it. They looked Egyptian, but

Gracie didn't know enough to understand what they said.

"Do we have tears?" Apep asked, his voice amused as she was dragged to stand in the middle of the designs with him. "Come now, this is a great honor."

The vampires released her, and Gracie immediately tried to run. Her feet hit the ground only twice before Apep's arms lashed out and wrapped around her waist. She screamed, throwing her head back against his chest, but she could have been a bunny licking his ears for all the response she got. Apep dragged her back to the center of the designs and spun her around. His hands clenched over her wrists, holding her in the spot no matter how she fought against him.

"Light it," he said over his shoulder.

Guinevere and Typhoon stood right behind him, the anger and hatred clear on their faces; both of them took a torch in a hand and stepped forward. Their jaws were clenched so tight that Gracie was certain they were holding back everything they wanted to say.

"Wait," she cried desperately as they lowered the torches to the outer ring. "Please! At least tell me what you're going to do to me. Please. I might only be some human to you, somebody you can drain dry, but I at least deserve to know why you're doing this."

Apep grunted, but that was enough for Typhoon and Guinevere to pause. They glanced at her and then him, waiting. Apep stared down at her, his monstrous size making her shudder; even if she had some sort of weapon, what could she do to him?

Knee him between the legs.

She'd hold off on that; wait to see if he would talk first.

To her relief, he did.

"What do you know about Ra?" Apep asked, cocking his head to one side.

Gracie swallowed roughly. Now that there was a lull, she wasn't certain if she could speak past the lump in her dry throat. She swallowed hard, coughed, and answered in a whisper. "I know that he was the head Egyptian god. He's supposed to be the sun... or a dung beetle that rolls the sun across the sky... something like that. I know that he's your enemy. The one story I read was that you were born from his umbilical cord..."

"Did it now?" Apep laughed and released one of her wrists. She fought the urge to bolt at once—he still had a grip on her, and if she attempted escape now, he'd only tighten his grip on her. She trembled with the urge to fight and flee but held herself back. Apep tapped her nose, causing her to flinch. "That is quite a story. Completely untrue but quite a story."

"It was thousands of years ago. All we have is records from a culture that has changed dramatically since its beginnings. So... what does Ra have to do with this?"

Apep smirked. "Ra was my enemy, as you said. We were both chosen by the other gods to receive unique gifts. I became the first vampire, and he the first shifter. But he swayed the others to his side, and rather than join me in my strength, they followed after him. Chose to be shifters. Have you not wondered why vampires can't stray into the light without drinking shifter blood?"

She hadn't even known that and remained silent.

"And yet, if a vampire drinks too much from a shifter, they will become a shifter. The final slap in my face, even after he killed me."

"How could he have killed you if you're alive now?"

"I'm a god. Death cannot hold me." Apep smiled. "You are a descendant of Ra. I see the light he so loved in your eyes. And since he took all from me, I will take all from him. I am in need of a goddess, and the old ones have all fallen to slumber… not that I'd want any of those wenches anyway. And you… when Ra is blood bound to me, I will be more powerful than he ever dreamed of being."

Gracie's breath caught in her throat. In need of a goddess? Bound by blood? Her stomach cramped as she shied back. Bile churned, and she suddenly felt fury welling up in her. She managed to rip her arm away as she kicked out; her knee crushed between Apep's legs; his eyes went wide as he bent over, letting out a groan of pain.

So even a god was vulnerable.

She didn't wait around to gloat. Instead, she turned on her heel and dashed away. The other vampires closed in around her; one of them grabbed her by the hair and yanked her backward. Her feet jerked out from under her and she fell heavily; something cracked, but whether it was her bones or the twigs beneath her she didn't know. All the air was driven from her lungs and she tried to gasp in vain.

There was a savage snarl, and the next thing Gracie knew, the vampire that had yanked her like that was on the ground, twitching and seizing. Typhoon stood over her and tossed the vampire's head aside. Gracie closed her eyes, choking on vomit even as she couldn't breathe.

The sound of a fist hitting flesh, followed by Typhoon's grunt of pain, only made her curl in tighter to herself. Her lungs were just starting to heave, her chest contracting rapidly as she tried to expel the vomit from her mouth and throat. Gentle hands turned her to her stomach and rubbed her back in soothing patterns. Guinevere's soft voice whispered in her ear, but she couldn't hear the words over Apep and Typhoon.

"He injured the girl; you said to kill anybody who attempted to keep her from you," Typhoon snarled out.

"She is not so badly injured." Another thump, another grunt of pain. Gracie coughed up the vomit then inhaled a gasping breath.

When she looked up, Apep stood over Typhoon, who was on his knees with his head bowed. His whole body shook, his hands clenched into fists. Gracie's eyes widened; he wasn't as completely controlled as the others thought. She could see him struggling to break free. If they could get him far enough from Apep, maybe he would—

Apep turned to her; he grabbed her by the back of the neck and dragged her to her feet, then pulled her back to the center of the carved stone. Two other vampires lit them, and flames burst up all around them. Apep clutched her to his chest, pulled her head to one side, and sank his fangs into her neck.

Oddly, there was no pain… at first.

When it hit, it was harder than having the wind knocked out of her. All the strength fled. Her muscles went limp as agony thrashed through her. Her vision blacked out and she could feel her blood draining, sucked out by great, greedy gulps. Apep's hands dug into her flesh. Her eyes rolled wildly as her jaw dropped open, but no sound came out.

Apep grunted, clutching her even tighter. Small growls emanated from his throat, his fingers bruising her.

Abruptly, he released her. She dropped, the pain still coursing through her. There was nothing else. She couldn't feel the ground below, nor the scorching heat of the flames that surrounded them. Only when Apep grasped her arm again could she feel anything.

A scream burst from her throat. Apep brought her to a sitting position and all the light and color burst around her. The monster vampire chuckled as he clasped a hand to her neck, firm enough to almost cut out her breathing. Something hot and wet ran down her chest and for a terrified moment she thought he was drooling on her; but no, it was her blood. Her head spun as she looked up at Apep's dark, pitiless eyes.

"Can you feel it? The venom sweeping through your blood? Soon you will have the greatest gift, Gracie Underhill. You will be immortal. You will stand by my side forever as my queen and goddess. You will be revered by all. That is..." He chuckled again. "If you survive the transformation. Let's hope you're stronger than the others."

He dropped her and strode through the flames, as though they had no effect on him. Something crackled, and a burst of fire ran along another line of the design, lighting a circle closer to her. Gracie screamed as white-hot pain shot through her body. She tried to jerk away from the flames, but they were all around her, their heat almost as painful as the venom coursing through her body.

"I hope you survive," Apep mused from behind the wall of flames. "If you do, that means I will, at last, have my goddess to start a new form of vampire. I have so long dreamt of everything I can do with this form... I hope that I can fulfill my fantasies with your form, too."

Once she was a vampire, she'd be under his sway. Like Guinevere. Like the rest of them. She wouldn't be able to fight back.

That was more terrifying than becoming a vampire. She lifted her head, white blinding her from the flames. An idea started to trickle into her mind... They weren't consuming her yet, just inching ever closer. He planned to burn her, just not yet. If she could just roll into the flames, perhaps their heat would kill her before the transformation began...

Daniel's face floated into her mind. His kind eyes, his crooked smile, the way he laughed when she made a silly pun. She closed her eyes and tried to imagine the warmth of his embrace. If only she could see him one last time...

But there was no time for dreams.

No time for wishes.

A tear rolled down her cheek and sizzled away.

Gracie threw herself into the heart of the flames. Apep roared. Pain burst through her as the flames licked over her skin. And then the sound of howling.

Chapter Eleven

Storm

Apep roared with laughter. Daniel couldn't see Gracie anymore, but the screams tore at his heart. He couldn't sit still anymore. He threw back his head and howled the command to attack, then dashed forward. The first two vampires he encountered weren't prepared; he ripped the arm off one and threw the other into a group of other vamps.

To his left, Mia and Shadow dashed out of the trees, quickly bringing down and mauling the vampires in their way. Thunder and Josef quickly split the vamps, breaking them into more manageable groups while Tornado, Andy and Stewart began to tear them apart. Daniel's gaze was solely on Apep. He reached through the flames to drag

Gracie from them, and Daniel leapt into the air.

His paws crashed into Apep's chest. Gracie fell limply to the ground, still half in the fire. Daniel's teeth clenched around Apep's arm. He dug his claws into Apep's chest and gave a mighty wrench. The vampire screamed in pain, but Daniel was already flinging the arm away. He whirled back, seizing Gracie's arm in his mouth and pulled her from the fire. The dress she wore was soaked in blood, her skin marble-white, no sign of burning or damage from the fire. Her head lolled to one side. Daniel shifted back to human form and gathered her into his arms.

"Gracie," he whispered, then his head jerked up as he heard a snarl.

Typhoon had broken through the barriers and was advancing; his muscles were tense as he stalked closer. “Idiot! You have a chance; don’t waste time!”

Daniel gently lowered Gracie, then lunged for Apep, who caught him in his hand… the hand Daniel had torn off. Daniel yelped in surprise as Apep threw him over his shoulder. He grunted as he impacted the ground, rolling off the edge of the exposed rock. He leapt back to his feet, a growl in his throat. Apep moved his arm experimentally as Daniel glanced to the side, where he had tossed the severed limb; it was still there.

A chill swept through him. Apep could regenerate himself.

The vampire laughed, holding up a hand to stop Typhoon from leaping at Daniel. “I am immortal,” he crowed. “I am a *god.* Did you think you could kill me? Even Ra himself could not end me. What makes you think you, a pitiful little child, could?"

"We'll see about that." Daniel lunged at Apep.

Typhoon stood off to one side, rocking back and forth on his heels. Apep sidestepped Daniel, laughed, and gestured at Typhoon. He turned on his heel and dashed in to attack Roxy, only to be attacked himself by Josef and Stewart. Daniel turned more slowly, hating Apep's smirk but knowing that if he just attacked it wouldn't benefit him. He had to play this smart.

"Done letting others do your dirty work, are you?" he growled, stepping to one side, studying Apep's body language. His shoulders were relaxed, a superior smile on this face and a look in his eye that said he was going to enjoy this. "Decided that you don't need to let others handle it for once?"

"Do you think your little taunts will affect me?" Apep laughed. "Look at your lover, boy. I have claimed her. Soon she will be mine. She will be a vampire and my goddess. See how the flames didn't scorch her? I was right... she is the one."

Daniel lunged again. His fist flew at Apep's face, but Apep easily sidestepped. Then sidestepped again. And again. When he struck, Daniel didn't even see his hand—but he felt it collide with his throat. He was tossed back, almost landing in the fire, next to Gracie's still body. He coughed, choked, and tried to draw in a breath through his bruised throat.

"What did you hope for, pup?" Apep taunted as he sidled forward. "Did you think you could rescue your Gracie and kill me? You should have known you were too weak for that."

Daniel's heart pounded. He could hear his people letting out cries of pain now; the vampires were rebounding, and Typhoon... He closed his eyes briefly. Apep was clearly stronger than him—he couldn't compete in brute strength.

"Don't worry about her, though. I won't force her into my bed. No, when I have her, she'll be begging me to fuck her."

There was only one thing to do. Daniel shifted back to his wolf form and barked out the commands to retreat. Then he seized Gracie, flung her to hang limply over his back, and dashed through the flames, away from Apep. Vampires turned, Apep let out a surprised shout, but the other shifters gathered around him and together they fled back into the forest.

They had run for a good ten minutes before Typhoon caught up. He batted Frieda aside and dug his claws into Daniel's flank.

Daniel stumbled to one side, Gracie slipping off his back. Shadow went for her; Daniel growled out a warning at her even as he whirled and head-butted Typhoon. Stewart and Andy came after the former alpha at both sides. Shadow snarled, then grabbed Gracie by the arm and threw her over Mia's back. The tiger let out a pained sound, causing Typhoon's head to whip around. For the briefest second, there was stillness all around.

Then Tornado dodged in and sank his teeth into Typhoon's shoulder, Mia dashed off with Gracie on her back, and vampires dropped in from the sky. Daniel fought hard, trying desperately not to see their faces. Teeth sank into his body; the scent of his blood filled the air. Then Typhoon was at him again.

Daniel clashed with the former Alpha, not holding back. Snarls and blood and fur flew. Typhoon fought as though he was possessed, ripping at Daniel's face and shoulders. Thunder, Tornado, and Blizzard all came at them and tackled Typhoon to the ground. Daniel stopped fighting to reorient himself even as he turned and latched on to the nearest vampire. As soon as he had some breathing room he looked quickly around, desperately searching for Guinevere.

He found her and Andy fighting, Andy trying to defend himself while Guinevere snarled and bit and scratched. Andy's foot slipped. He went down, Guinevere falling after him. Daniel's heart left his throat as his father howled in pain while his mother's teeth sink into his neck. She tore back, blood pouring down her chin. At once, her hands closed around her mate's neck and began to choke the life from him. Daniel rushed forward but was blocked by half a dozen more vampires.

"Get away," she screamed even as Andy fought to break her hold. "Don't look!"

He was too far away. Cold, hollow dread filled him. He tried desperately to get to them; he tore through vampires. He ripped them apart and tossed pieces behind in his wake. But Andy's movements were slowing, becoming jerkier. He couldn't get there in time.

And then Stewart was there. He leapt onto Guinevere's back, his teeth sinking into her shoulder as he yanked her back. She cried out in pain as she was torn away. Roxy darted in, grabbing her leg. Bone snapped as she wrenched her head one way then the other. Guinevere collapsed as Stewart and Roxy grabbed Andy's twitching body and dragged him away from the fight, disappearing into the trees.

Typhoon rammed into his side. Daniel stumbled, rolled over and snapped his jaws over the alpha's leg. He jerked, pulling Typhoon off balance. The majority of the vampires disappeared into the trees, with screeches heard between the foliage, to find Gracie. The other shifters broke free from their battles; They chased after the vampires, leaving Daniel and Typhoon alone.

The former alpha freed himself from Daniel's jaws, stumbling away. Daniel took the opportunity to roll to his feet and dash blindly into the trees. Satisfaction swept through him, then he concentrated on maintaining the distance between himself and Typhoon; close enough to continue luring him alone, but just out of reach.

He ran for some time, until his sides were heaving and slick with sweat. The sound of Typhoon crashing through the trees was growing more distant, so Daniel picked his spot and turned. Within seconds, the alpha charged through the brush. He attempted to skid to a stop when he saw Daniel had changed his tactics, but his bleeding leg caught on a log and he tumbled head over heels, landing with a painful crash.

Daniel was on him in an instant, using his bulk to pin the bigger wolf to the forest floor. He closed his jaws around Typhoon's throat and Typhoon froze. Daniel let out a growl.

Beneath him, the huge wolf's body shifted to human. Daniel hesitated only a second before he shifted as well; wasn't this what he wanted, a chance to talk with Typhoon? He only prayed that they were far enough from Apep that his control was weakened.

Typhoon glowered at him as Daniel continued to pin him down, this time putting a knife he'd strapped to his leg against Typhoon's neck to keep him in place. Behind the glower, Typhoon almost seemed… pleased.

"I think you know what this means," Daniel snarled at him. "I am tired of you hunting us constantly. It's time for it to end."

Was that relief in Typhoon's eyes? "Good," he growled out. "Because I'm tired of being a puppet. And you can't take me prisoner."

Daniel tried to keep his face blank as he realized Typhoon expected him to kill him; it had been his intention to take him prisoner. Could he really kill the former alpha? Outside of his father and uncles, Typhoon had taught him more about life than anybody else… he was the only one who understood what it meant to be half shifter, half vampire!

"I don't like being told what to do," he settled on. "And besides that, I don't relish the thought of what Mia would do to me if I killed you."

Typhoon's eyes widened, then narrowed. He hissed out a laugh. "You're a fool, then. I am a danger, your enemy; if you can't kill me, how do you expect to protect her?"

Daniel stared down at him and lost his focus for a split second as his mind turned to Gracie; that split second was all Typhoon needed. He buckled his body, tossing Daniel off to the side. His fist hit Daniel's wrist and the knife went flying. Typhoon snarled as he pounced on Daniel, pinning him down. His hands wrapped around Daniel's throat as he started to squeeze.

"We all have orders to kill you if we get the chance," Typhoon snarled. "You've gotten closer to killing him than any of the others. If you had kept your focus, you could have killed him! We could all be free! And now I'm going to kill you and there is nothing either of us can do to stop it."

Daniel punched him in the kidneys, but it didn't seem to have any effect. He grappled with the hands squeezing his neck. His breath choked off and he could feel his pulse thrumming against Typhoon's fingers. Panic started to rise in him even as he tried to force it down. He wasn't going to give up without a fight!

His fingers raked down Typhoon's arms, across his face, everywhere he could reach. Blood oozed from the wounds, but Typhoon didn't seem to notice, his eyes hard and angry, his teeth bared in a snarl. Darkness started to swirl before Daniel's eyes.

Then Mia's voice rang out. "Robbie!"

Typhoon's head jerked up. He began trembling as his grip loosed just enough for Daniel to gasp in a noisy breath.

"Robbie," Mia repeated, her voice softer. "Don't..."

"Mia," Typhoon choked out, as though he was the one being strangled now. "You can't... you have to go."

She moved forward, her hands outstretched. "Come home. Please. You can fight him. I know you're stronger than this."

Typhoon snarled so violently that Mia flinched back. Daniel lay as still as he could, trying to regain his strength before he brought Typhoon's attention back to him. After what seemed like forever, Mia started to inch forward again, her eyes pleading as tears ran down her face.

"You're stronger than him," she whispered. "You can fight him."

"I can't," Typhoon choked out. "I can't... You have to leave. He's ordered me to kill you and I... I'm not strong enough."

"You are," Mia whispered.

Typhoon suddenly lunged. Daniel reached for his ankle, his nails digging into Typhoon's skin; Typhoon shifted even as he went after her. One paw whacked her hard in the head, and then

Typhoon was off. He howled as he dashed through the trees, where to, Daniel didn't know. Daniel wanted to rush after him, but Mia was collapsed on the ground, her hand clutched to her face as she sobbed.

Daniel hurried to her side and lifted her from the ground. *He's strong enough to run rather than fight,* he thought desperately as he listened to Typhoon's cries fade away. His thoughts turned to his mother and he flinched. *Maybe there is hope after all...*

Chapter Twelve

Gracie

Blood.

It was all around her, seeping into the air like something alive, wafting around her in a seductive dance. Her throat burned so hotly it felt like there was a fire inside of her, a fire that could only be sated by the sweet, warm taste of blood. She longed for it to run hot and thick down her throat... her desires made her feel sick to her stomach, but when Daniel bent over her, putting his neck close to her mouth, she couldn't help but lunge, trying to sink her fangs into him.

He yanked back just in time, as thick leather bands wrapped around her, pinning her in place. Mia rushed around shouting orders, but Gracie couldn't understand what she was saying over the pulsing of her blood in her ears. A fresh wave of agony burst over her and she bent her back, fighting the restraints as she screamed. Daniel's scent filled her nostrils as he smoothed her hair and whispered in her ear.

His scent... the scent of his blood. She longed for a taste and stretched her neck, trying to reach him. Just one little bite, one little taste... that would ease the burning in her throat and might even numb the waves of pain that kept coming over her.

"We need to give her blood." Daniel's voice broke through everything else. "She's turning, if she doesn't get blood—"

"I know," Mia snapped. "I need to take care of Twister first."

Turning. Gracie started to shake from her head to her toes as she realized what that meant. Apep had bitten her. She was becoming a vampire. Then she'd be under his control. He'd be able to do whatever he wanted with her. She'd be his unwilling goddess, the one standing next to him as he completed his plans to take over the world.

"No," she cried, her fighting renewed even though she couldn't move an inch. Daniel's face swam through the tears in her eyes. "No, don't let me become a vampire. Please! I don't want to be a vampire. Don't let it happen, please. Don't let me become a vampire. I don't want to be his goddess!"

"You won't be." Daniel's voice was soothing, even for the tinge of fear in it. "I promise. I won't let that happen. Just hold in there, Gracie. I'll look after you. I promise."

"Don't let me become a vampire," she begged again, hoping he'd understand what she meant—if necessary, she'd rather die.

Something touched her lips. It was hot and wet. The scent of blood increased, and her eyes widened even as she latched onto whatever it was. The tang hitting her tongue was blissful; she moaned in rapture as she sucked in that sweet, sweet liquid. The burning in her throat cooled, and the next ripple of pain to wash over her body wasn't as intense, and a triumphant smile spread over her face. She'd been right—

Then the realization that she was drinking blood hit her and she recoiled with a cry of disgust. Daniel was still bent over her. Blood rushed down an open wound in his wrist and she realized that she had been drinking directly from him.

"Daniel," she started, her tone pleading.

He kissed her forehead and smoothed her hair from her face. "It's going to be okay. I promise. Shifter blood makes a vampire turn more human, it might be able to stop your transformation altogether."

She moaned, hoping he was right but not daring to ask what if he was wrong. A savage snarl beside her made her jerk and cry out, her body responding automatically to the threat. Her head twisted around, and she saw Twister. He was strapped down like she was, his muscles bulging as he tried to rip himself free. They were in a darkened room; Gracie didn't know how they had gotten here, she had been too out of it to pay attention to her surroundings.

Twister let out a stream of strangled curses. Foam bubbled at his lips and his nails were claws. Mia bustled around him, stringing IVs to him and then, with Roxy and Cyclone holding his head, she shoved a long tube down his nose. He coughed, gasped, and snarled out something Gracie couldn't understand.

"This is the last of our vampire blood," Mia said as she hooked a dark red bag up to flow through the tube in Twister's nose. "I only hope it's enough."

Why were they giving him vampire blood? Gracie opened her mouth to ask, but even as she did so, Mia turned to her. The tiger shifter's eyes were cold as she grabbed a second tube and motioned for Daniel to hold Gracie's head still. She yelped in protest, but Mia eased the tube down her nose. It rubbed her burning throat raw and she cried out.

"We have to get lots of shifter blood into you," Daniel explained as Mia hooked up another blood bag, this one much brighter in color, to run down into Gracie's stomach. Daniel kissed her forehead again. "Try to stay still, love."

Love? With everything else going on, Gracie almost missed it. She gaped at him, a feeling that she had no name for starting to bubble up through her chest. It was warm but not the burning sensation that had accompanied the hunger in her throat. She tried to lift a hand, not to lash out like before but to touch Daniel's face. She didn't dare speak, though. Not with the tube in her throat.

Twister let out a particularly loud howl and Roxy put her hands on his chest, rubbing him in circular patterns with a look of fear and anger on her face. What must it be like to watch your younger brother go through something like that? Gracie shuddered as she shrank back in on herself. They were only in this situation because of her... because they had rescued her.

Somewhere behind them, Blizzard growled. "If she becomes a vampire, you know what we have to do. We can't risk—"

"Giving up a source of fresh vampire blood?" Shadow interrupted. "Yeah, my first thought was to kill her, too. But we don't have any more vampire blood and we can't exactly go collect more from the blood bank. If she turns, we will have to utilize the resource she presents."

Gracie cried out, trying to tell them no. The tube constricted her throat and she coughed, choking and gasping. Mia rushed over and checked the tube before snarling out. "Don't try to talk. We're doing all we can to prevent you from turning. If you do turn, it's like Shadow says. We'll have to utilize the resource."

Gracie shook her head, tears in her eyes.

"You'd be too much of a risk to keep around constantly," Mia assured her. "After we got the blood we needed, we'd kill you."

Daniel snarled, so loud and deep that she could feel it reverberate through her chest. Some part of her shied away at once, but oddly enough a sense of calm went through her at the same time. Daniel was with her. He was looking after her. It didn't matter what happened, so long as he was by her side. Her fingers stretched out, brushing against his, and he pulled her hand tightly into his.

"I will not allow her to be killed," Daniel said staunchly. "Not any more than I will allow my mother or Typhoon to be killed. Nor will I allow my father to die, either. We give her the shifter blood and hopefully, that will stop the transformation. If it doesn't, if she becomes a vampire, then I am damn well going to go back and tear Apep apart piece by piece. He's not going to take the people I love away from me!"

There was that word again. Gracie strained against the leather bounds. She opened her mouth, wanting to ask him if that meant what she thought it did.

But even before she remembered the tube going down her throat, a blast of white-hot agony washed through her. Her body buckled. She spasmed and convulsed. Then everything went black.

***

It felt like there was a stake being driven through her heart. It grew sharper every time she inhaled, so she tried not to breathe at all. The room was overly hot, making her tongue feel dry. Her body ached, but it was nothing compared to that singular pain in her chest. She groaned, trying to adjust her position and hopefully ease it. A hand smoothed over her forehead and she flinched from the contact.

"Sorry," Daniel murmured.

Relief washed over her as she faced him again. A small smile came over her face as the pain faded a little more. When she opened her mouth, she realized that the burning pain was no longer there. Her throat was raw and dry, but she could breathe just fine. The tube must have been taken out.

"Hey," she murmured, her voice cracking hoarsely.

"Drink this."

He held a cup to her mouth, the little straw pointed toward her. She took a couple of sips before the tangy, sweet flavor registered. She gagged, trying to spit the blood back out, but Daniel shook his head.

"I know you don't want to, but you have to try to drink, okay?"

She thought about asking why, but instead obediently drank. The pain in her chest faded away entirely and she rested her head back, feeling utterly exhausted even for having just woken up. Her eyes started to close but then snapped back open. She turned her head, seeking Daniel out again with a questioning look.

"Did the shifter blood work?"

He hesitated, and her stomach plummeted. "It slowed your transformation. But we don't think it will halt it entirely. The best we can hope for is controlling the way you change, so you won't have any uncontrollable urges."

Tears flooded her vision. "I don't want to be a vampire."

"I know." He kissed her forehead. "But really, it's not as bad as you might think. My mother's been a vampire for centuries and she has a good handle on it. Bloodlust is a danger that you have to be wary of, but as long as you don't let yourself get too hungry, it's not something that you'll have to worry about. Plus, a steady diet of shifter blood will keep you more human than vampire. All is not lost."

Gracie wanted to believe him. She wanted to accept what he was saying and think nothing else about it. But the thoughts that had been running through her head before flooded back and she started to cry, even as she fought her tears.

"Apep wants me as his goddess. He turned me into a vampire so he can control my every action. I'll be a danger to you and the others. I can't... I can't be a vampire, Daniel! I can't. I'd rather—" She cut herself off, shuddering. Would she really rather be dead? If it meant she wasn't under Apep's control, if it meant she was free of whatever he planned for her... yes. But would she rather be dead than a vampire? Especially with the precautions Daniel had just said they could take? She took a shuddering breath and reached for his hand. To her surprise, she found she was no longer strapped down. She wondered, briefly, if it was safe, but Daniel would know how to take care of himself. "Thank you. For saving me."

"Of course," Daniel's eyes burned. "I could never leave you in his hands."

"Is Twister alright?"

Daniel nodded. "Yeah. Aunt Roxy and Uncle Stewart are with him now... I wanted to stay with you."

What he had said before she went unconscious went through her mind. Love. Was it really possible? Could he... love her? She was too nervous to ask. If he did, what would she say in response?

"Gracie...." He leaned forward, looking hesitant as he met her gaze. "There is something I want to ask you. It's going to be uncomfortable and I'll understand if you want to tell me to fuck off."

Dread dropped into her stomach, but she nodded, encouraging him to continue.

"Your blood did something for Apep. I have to wonder... I mean, I'm half vamp... Maybe it will do the same for me."

Gracie's eyes widened. He wanted to drink her blood? She didn't know how to respond to that. Part of her shrank back... but another part of her told her to go for it. She stared at him, seeing the hesitation in his eyes, seeing how uncertain he was. She thought of the pain that had poured through her when Apep drank from her... and somehow knew that it would not be the same with him.

She swallowed hard, then nodded and tilted her head to one side, exposing her throat to him. Daniel leaned forward. His tongue flicked over her pulse, making a shudder run through her, and then twin pricks sent a gasp rushing through her. Then he was drinking... and heat burned through her body. Her core tightened as she clung to him, a snarl on her own lips as the pleasure built higher.

Chapter Thirteen

Storm

Blood was never something he craved. Sure, from time to time he felt himself getting weaker in one way or another and knew it was time to step up his hemoglobin. Even then, though, it was a chore to choke down straight blood. But Gracie's... Gracie's blood was like the sweetest nectar. The only thing sweeter was the nectar between her legs when he brought her to climax.

Waves of pleasure washed through him as he finished into her with a couple thrusts, then licked the tiny holes in her neck where he'd been drinking. Gracie did the same, gently cleaning the area she had been drinking from him. After two weeks, the transformation had completed; if she stopped drinking his blood for any solid length of time, she would become full vampire. Fortunately, it seemed like her steady diet of shifter blood kept her human enough to prevent Apep from taking control of her.

Daniel nestled into her neck, loving the scent of her, and he slowly withdrew from the heat of her core. Gracie let out a sigh of disappointment. He chuckled and kissed her lightly, the mingled taste of their blood on their mouths. Gracie wrapped her arms around him, tracing her fingers down his back where she had been clawing earlier.

She grimaced. "I hope I didn't hurt you. I still don't know how strong I am."

"Darling, that was anything but painful."

A rapid pounding on the door made them both groan. Shadow

shouted, “You’d better be finished. We’re leaving in ten minutes. Be ready or get left behind.”

The two of them glanced at each other, grimaced, and reluctantly climbed out of bed. This was the best place they had been so far, and it was going to be difficult to leave it. Not only was there room for everybody to have their own space, but the walls were thick enough that the two of them didn’t have to worry about disturbing others when they made love.

Best of all? Locks on the doors. So none of the children could walk in on them, leading to some very awkward conversations.

They pulled on their clothing, sighing once more. Daniel was tempted to delay a little, but that would set a dangerous precedent. After he had stepped up and taken command of the leftover leadership of the Brotherhood in order to save Gracie, he had become firmly entrenched as the leader. That wasn't to say he wasn't without challenges, but he had been able to meet every one that was thrown at him and come forward with a glint in his eye and the support of the other former alphas.

It seemed that he had been right from the start... somebody needed to step up and take the leadership, rather than waiting for everybody to agree on it.

Since rescuing Gracie, they had been constantly on the move. Apep's attacks were more frequent, and so Melanie, Ava, Roxy, Mia, and Blizzard had taken the children and found a good underground location, far from the immediate threat. Apep didn't seem interested in them, only Daniel and Gracie. He himself hadn't come after them—Daniel had to wonder if it meant he was afraid of them somehow—and Typhoon hadn't been seen either. The sheer number of vampires that were constantly hunting them, though, was enough that they couldn't stay in any location longer than it took to get a rest and fill their bellies.

For all that, though, things had never looked better. Daniel had hacked the media more than once, sending messages all across the country calling members of the Savage Brotherhood to gather and fight. He encouraged the humans to fight back, too, and there had been more than one riot reported. Vampires were struggling to hold onto their populations, and more and more people were flocking to the cause of defeating Apep once and for all.

"Hurry up," Shadow shouted as she moved off.

Gracie rolled her eyes as she pulled her shirt on. "We're already packed and ready to go, what more does she want?"

"Probably to be on the bikes already," Daniel replied with a wink. "She's a good beta to have. I understand why Tornado was so successful at his young age."

Gracie rolled her eyes once more. "You're one to talk about young ages. God! I can't think about that, it's too weird."

Daniel chuckled. He grabbed his pack and Gracie's as he waited for her to put on her shoes. It was true enough that she still had a difficult time with his age, but in the end, he'd convinced her that it didn't mean anything except for a small lack in actual experience. It didn't change the fact that he was an adult just as much as she was. He had done a full kindergarten to high school education in his first year of life, proving that his brain was a quick learner, so he wasn't undereducated, either.

Gracie took her pack and slid it onto her back as they left. Tornado and Thunder were already waiting at the bikes, loading up their provisions, while Josef, Andy, and Stewart all were making sure the tanks were topped off. Frieda was on her phone, having a quietly murmured conversation. Her gaze flashed over to them, and she gave them a strained smile.

Shadow snorted as they started to secure their packs to the backs of their bikes. She was already ready to go, her fingers tapping against the one handle of her bike. Daniel ignored her impatience. This was going to be a riskier move; since vampires no longer seemed to be bound to stay out of the sunshine, the gang traveled at night, so as to avoid the gazes of humans who might turn them in. They were going to meet with another group of shifters who were fighting the good fight but being rather clumsy at it; Daniel was going to give them strategies and leave Thunder with them as their alpha, before heading out again.

"Change of plans," Frieda announced as she walked to her bike, slipping her phone back into her pocket.

"Sorry, but I shall not be going with you anymore."

Daniel frowned at his aunt. He couldn't stop the annoyance from slipping into his voice. "And why is that? You have something better to do?"

Frieda gave him an apologetic look. "I don't want to go and sit around doing nothing, but circumstances have changed. That was Mia and she was just giving me the results of some tests that we took before we separated. Turns out that I'm pregnant."

Stewart dropped a wrench, which clattered noisily to the floor. He dashed over to her, picking her up and whirling in the air. "Are you fucking serious?"

"Yes," Frieda yelped, then laughed as she started kissing him. "And I have to get to the others, because I can't risk—"

"Of course," Shadow grunted. She shook her head, but there was a smile tugging at her lips which belayed the annoyance she was trying to show. "Get yourself knocked up and leave us to do the fighting. Typical. I'll have you know that I never took a day off when I was pregnant."

Frieda shot her an annoyed glance. "Don't give me that bullshit. I know Tornado kept you out of the field when you were preggers."

Shadow shrugged but grinned. Everybody moved forward, clapping Stewart and Frieda on their backs and offering their congratulations. Daniel hung back until everyone else had moved aside, then embraced his aunt and uncle. This was good news—hope in the time when it seemed like all hope had been taken away from them. Still, it wasn't without its risks. It was more important now than ever that they figure out how to retrieve Typhoon and Guinevere, that they make a plan to finally take out Apep once and for all.

Daniel had no idea how they were going to do that. All he knew was it had to be done.

"Uncle Stewart, Dad," he turned to Stewart and Andy both. "I want you to escort Aunt Frieda to the others. We'll meet up in Adamsvale."

Andy gripped his shoulder briefly, worry shining from his eyes. Daniel knew better than to think that it was because his father doubted him, though. Since Andy was bitten, he had been jumpier, and far more protective of Daniel, Stewart, and Frieda. He'd had a difficult time deciding to continue on with them, rather than staying with Roxy and the kids to protect them.

"I take it to mean you want me to stay with the group?" Josef asked, his voice even.

"Yes. I know you'd like to see Aunt Roxy and the kids, but I need you with us. You still have money and the rest of us..."

Josef nodded, struggling to keep the disappointment off his face. "Of course."

"Now." Daniel climbed onto his bike. "Let's get going. Safe travels, all."

***

The group in Adamsvale called themselves the Brotherhood United and contained several members of the Coalfell chapter. They welcomed Tornado warmly, and Daniel wondered if he ought to switch and leave him here rather than Thunder. He kept that at the back of his mind as he listened to what they had been doing, their successes and failures. When they told him that a large group of shifters were being held prisoner in a blood-processing factory, anger whirled through him.

One of the United members, the former barkeep named Lem, eyed Gracie with his nostrils flaring. “What is a vampire doing with you?”

“Gracie is immune to Apep’s control.” Daniel didn’t add that they didn’t know if she would succumb if she became less human or if Apep got too close. “He’s been coming after her since she was human, so I’m keeping her close.”

“Very close,” Lem muttered, nostrils flared again. He glared at Gracie this time. “What does Apep want with you?”

Gracie shrugged, looking unconcerned. “He wants to turn me into his goddess. Which is never happening.” She grinned, flashing her fangs. “He comes near me again and I’ll tear out his throat. He’ll see what happens when he messes with the children of Ra.”

Lem looked impressed and confused. Daniel smirked, then turned the conversation back to the prisoners. They had to rescue them, something Lem had tried to do several times to no avail.

"Shadow, you go scout out the prison. Find us a way in."

Tornado looked like he wanted to protest but said nothing. Shadow smirked and slipped away. The rest of them continued with the other things, including Josef forking over fistfuls of cash he'd managed to get from some of his offshore accounts—a stroke of luck, since the majority of his money had been confiscated by Apep's forces. What he'd managed to get was enough to fund them for a little while, but Daniel was already planning another heist. Who knew when it would run out?

Much later, after Shadow had returned and they put together a plan to rescue the prisoners, Gracie and Daniel retired to a little closet that would be serving as their bedroom. Both of them collapsed into their sleeping bags, too exhausted to think about lovemaking.

"'He'll see what happens when he messes with the children of Ra.'" Daniel chuckled. "That was nicely dramatic."

"Thanks. I've been working on it." Gracie groped in the darkness for his hand. "Do you think this plan will work?"

"It better." Daniel sighed and moved a little closer. "I fucking love you." There was silence, and Daniel suddenly felt very self-conscious. He cleared his throat and tried to fix it. "I mean, I love fucking you. With you. It's great and I—"

"I love you, too."

Warmth spread through his chest. A smile bloomed over his face and he turned, wrapping his arms around her. His exhaustion was forgotten as he kissed her over and over again. Gracie laughed as she returned his kisses, but suddenly stopped and pressed both hands to his chest.

"You'd better come back to me after you rescue those prisoners," she hissed. "Or else."

"You'd better be waiting for me." He kissed her. "Or else."

"I will be," Gracie sighed, and then neither of them spoke, as their mouths were busy doing other things.

Chapter Fourteen

Gracie

It had been an hour since Daniel left with the others to rescue the vampires' prisoners. Gracie wrapped bandages, trying to keep her hands busy as she stoutly refused to imagine what might be going on with the fighting. It was a rather hurried plan, after all, although Shadow had found several things Lem and the others hadn't known about.

Lem himself sat next to her, rearranging the medical supplies, putting them in proper order. He glanced at the clock and shook his head with a soft growl. "If I was a younger man, I'd have gone out with them. If I had known that vampires were going to start taking over the world, I never would have let myself get so soft."

Gracie glanced at him, with his white hair and lined face, and wondered how he had planned to stop himself from getting old. She shook her head as she set aside the bandages she was working on and started on the next bunch.

"I've never been much of a fighter," she told him. "I never thought I'd end up living in what's essentially a war zone. If I had known… I'd probably have had a mental breakdown."

Lem snorted, rolled his eyes and handed her another box of bandages. "You know, the reason I stopped going into the field was because I got too old to watch my friends die. It never gets easier… I never thought I'd have to sit around and wait for the kids I saw grow up die. It should be me out there… not some kid with a mate and children waiting for him to come home."

A pang hit Gracie in the stomach. She reached over to put a comforting hand on his shoulder. He tensed, and she flinched. Of course. She was a vampire. He was a shifter. He didn't want her touching him, even if he was kind enough to spend this time with her.

She withdrew, feeling her cheeks heating, and cleared her throat. "Sorry. But you're doing a good job here. Even if you're not in the fighting. I mean, I couldn't do all this by myself."

Especially since the others are all convinced that I'm going to go for their throats, she thought as she glanced around. A good dozen of the others looked away from their glares. She ducked her head and sighed.

"I didn't ask to be a vampire," she mumbled.

Lem didn't respond.

A chill stole over Gracie's skin, goosebumps forming on her arms. She shuddered and glanced up, her eyes seeking the doorways at once. Her heart, which barely had a beat now that she was a vampire, started to pound and her hands shook. Something was wrong… Something was *coming*.

She jumped to her feet and shouted a warning even as the windows shattered. Doors bust open and vampires poured into the building. The shifters leapt to meet them, shifting into a variety of forms as they did so. Gracie grabbed the nearest thing she could use as a weapon and smashed a vampire across the face as he went after Lem.

Did this mean that those who had gone to rescue the prisoners had been stopped? Daniel's face flashed through her mind and terror welled in her. If he'd been hurt... if he'd been killed...

Lem grabbed her arm and threw her back as a vampire lunged at her. She shook herself, sliding into a fighting position that Daniel had taught her. A vampire struck at her and she blocked the blow, then threw a clumsy punch which was easily dodged. As she fought, a well of frustration rose in her. Why? Why did it have to be this way?

She thought of Daniel again and a hatred for all the blood spilled choked her lungs.

She shouted before she had even realized the word was forming in her brain. "Stop!"

Howls, grunts, and then silence. The vampires had all frozen, and the shifters stared in confusion. A couple of the vampires tried to keep fighting, but it was as though their arms had turned into noodles; they couldn't seem to control themselves. Slowly, every gaze turned to her. Gracie stared around in shock, then swallowed hard.

"Go sit down over there," she pointed as she whispered, her throat dry.

Automatically, marching like tin soldiers, the vampires obeyed. Gracie pressed a hand to her mouth. What the hell...? How was this possible? Was that why Apep had said he would turn her into his goddess? Did he know...? Because she was a child of Ra, did that mean she could control the vampires just as much as him?

"No wonder he was so determined to get me," she breathed.

Lem stared at her with something like aw and horror. The rest of the shifters all glared at her, looking as confused as she felt. Gracie wiped her hands on her jeans and inched her way forward, keeping her gaze on the vampires sitting on the floor. The harder she stared at them, the more she saw. Faces lined with wariness. A resignation in some, defiance in others. All of them confused.

One of them finally spoke. "You're her."

Gracie turned to him.

"You're the one the Master wants. The daughter of Ra. The one that will make him unstoppable."

"Or the one to stop him," Gracie responded.

As she stared at the vampire, she saw something shimmering around him. Something that looked like red chains, wrapping around his throat, his chest, his hands. She reached out and was able to take them in her hands. As she did so, the burning need for blood that she had felt when she first was being turned flashed in her throat.

With a cry, she jerked away—the chains broke in her hands and the vampire gasped, eyes widening.

"What?" he breathed, reaching a trembling hand to his throat. He stared at her in confusion and wonder. "It's gone."

"What is?" she asked.

His jaw worked for a moment. “The… the bloodlust. It’s gone.”

Suddenly she understood. Looking at the others, she saw those same chains wrapped around them. It was the bloodlust of the vampire’s curse. Moving quickly, she moved to each of them and broke the chains. All of them cried out as she did so; once freed, they looked at her in amazement. Several started to cry even.

“I can’t hear his voice in my head anymore,” one of them said with a laugh. She jumped to her feet and stretched her arms. “You have saved us!”

“What the fuck?” Lem hissed.

Gracie turned to him and shook her head. “I don’t know. I guess… I guess I’m special after all. This must be why Apep was so determined to keep me at his side. Because I take their bloodlust away… and the bloodlust," she dug her hands into her hair, understanding. "It's how he controls them!"

The vampires stood, murmuring to each other as they looked at their own hands and each other in amazement. When Gracie turned back to them, several fell to their knees. The other shifters looked on in confusion and disgust, a few glaring at her distrustfully. One of the kneeling vampires took her hand and kissed it.

"Bless you, Lady. Bless you."

"Don't," Gracie said, flushing and uncomfortable with the attention when it was just coincidence she had managed to figure this all out. But they didn't stop, all moving forward to murmur their thanks and praise her. It wasn't until one of the shifters snarled that the tension increased once more.

Lem stepped up beside Gracie's shoulder. "If the bloodlust was what enabled Apep to control them, then I would suggest it was also what enabled you to control them. A child of Ra, huh?" He shook his head. "I should read up on all this crap. But we can't just let them hang out like this is a social occasion."

The first vampire who had kissed her hand shook his head. "We have no love of Apep. He's made us do things that we hated… and we hate him. Take us as your prisoners if you must, but allow us to stay. Please. We can help you in this fight. We want to see him dead as much as you."

Lem glared but nodded slowly. A few of the shifters cried out in protest, but Lem silenced them with a snarl. “Go lock them in the cellar. We’ll wait for Storm to return to tell us what to do with them… if what we think is happening here has happened… then we have got a weapon to use against Apep. For the first time since this bloody war started.”

***

Gracie worried and fretted for another few hours until Daniel and the others came back. She immediately flew into his arms, trying to blurt out the story in between kisses. Daniel wrapped his arms around her waist and silenced her with a hard kiss to her mouth. When he pulled back, she was so breathless that he was able to get his words in.

“Typhoon and Mom were there,” he said, his eyes bright. “And after we freed the vampires’ prisoners…”

He gestured behind him. Tornado, Josef, and Thunder dragged two unconscious forms between them. Typhoon and Guinevere.

Gracie squealed, her eyes brightening as she gazed at them. Those same chains that had wrapped around the other vampires were around them, too... but not around Daniel. He had told her that he didn't have the burning desire to drink blood that both his mother and Typhoon had warned him about... born without bloodlust, then?

She grinned as she strode forward and took hold of the chains wrapped tightly around Typhoon. "And this is something that I discovered while you were gone."

It was easy to break these chains, and they faded away to nothingness as she stepped back and told Daniel everything that had transpired. He stared at her as though she had told him that she was pregnant—shocked, excited, with a bit of disbelief thrown in there for good measure. It took a good while to explain everything to his satisfaction. And by that time, Typhoon and Guinevere had regained consciousness.

Guinevere sobbed as she wrapped her arms around Daniel, asking about Andy. Daniel reassured her, then explained what they had discovered. Typhoon stood by, his expression grim as he glanced around at the people who once called him a leader. He cleared his throat and stepped forward.

"Thank you," he said to Gracie. "I knew he feared you as much as he wanted you at his side. I never dreamt..."

He let out a shaky breath as his chin dropped to his chest. “I have never felt so… Free…” He swallowed and turned to Daniel. “Apep fears you, too.”

“You said,” Daniel murmured dryly. “Care to tell me why?”

“Because only a vampire-shifter hybrid can kill him. That was why he kept me so close, he didn’t want me breaking from his control… and when he found he couldn’t control you at all, it terrified him.”

Daniel nodded, his brow furrowing. Then a grin crossed his face and he held out his hand to Typhoon. “Well, then. Let’s show him what happens when he messes with the alphas of the Savage Brotherhood, shall we?”

Typhoon stared doubtfully for a moment before grinning back. “Yeah. Let’s show that bastard what we’re made of.”

Chapter Fifteen

Storm

There were far more survivors than Daniel expected. He had called for them all to gather together; with Typhoon recovered, they came flocking back. A few of them yelled at the former alpha for keeping his true heritage a secret, but all it took was a few snarls and glares from him to get those people to shut the hell up.

Now, he and Typhoon ran side-by-side, with Gracie between them as they dashed through the darkened hallways of Apep's center of power. If Apep thought that they'd be hindered by the darkness, he had another thing coming. The three of them could see as well in pitch black as the brightest day, and they'd equipped the rest of the Brotherhood with night vision goggles.

That was all it took for them to run their raid.

Daniel's blood surged with adrenaline as he, Gracie and Typhoon ran through a horde of vampires, held back by a plethora of shifters who had opened the way for them. Snarls and screams filled the air, the taste of blood heavy and the scent of fear trickling down the walls. Gracie slowed, and Typhoon snarled a warning, but then she stopped altogether.

"The chains," she murmured, more to herself than them. "They're all connected here. He's woven them so tightly in his grasp..."

Typhoon snarled again, but Daniel let out a short bark; yes, the plan was for them to take down Apep which would hopefully stop all the vampires from being forced to follow out his control—but wouldn't it be better if they had more fighters on their side? The vampires Gracie had freed already were fighting alongside the shifters, just as fierce as any of the Brotherhood in opening the passage for the three of them to get to Apep.

Gracie didn't waste time trying to convince Typhoon as he cricked his tail in annoyance. Her hands reached out, a sort of golden glow haloing her as her face twisted in concentration.

She yanked hard, and then it was as though something yanked her back; her feet slipped out from under her as a roar rushed down the hallway. An invisible force dragged her along. Daniel yelped and leapt after her, Typhoon on their heels. It wasn't long before she slipped into the crowd of vampires.

Daniel didn't let himself stop and doubt; he threw himself over the heads of the shifters, crashing through the vampires as he followed Gracie's scent.

Typhoon snarled as he plunged in after them. Claws and fangs tore at them from all sides, but together the two fought hard, working their way through the horde until they caught sight of Apep, standing much taller than everyone else. He had Gracie by the throat with one hand, his face twisted in anger and hatred.

He let out a bark just before shifting to human form; Typhoon seized him in his jaws and hurled him over the heads of the vampires. Several of them reached out to grab him, shouting.

Apep looked up just in time from Daniel's feet to collide with his face. He yelled, his grip loosening enough on Gracie for her to break free. She pressed herself against the wall, coughing as Daniel bounced back to his feet and shifted, going for Apep's throat. Apep sidestepped, only to come into Typhoon's path. The alpha seized him by the leg and yanked his head hard to one side. Daniel darted in, seizing Apep around the middle. They yanked in opposite directions. Apep's fists flew out; one slammed into Daniel's face, sending him backward. Several vampires surrounded Gracie, and she tore her hands through the air, glowing brighter and brighter like the sun.

With a howl, Apep whipped around and bit into Typhoon's shoulder. Daniel lunged forward, having to trust Gracie would be able to handle her vampires; several of them were falling to their knees already, gasping as though drawing breath for the first time. He concentrated on Apep, darting in and tearing off strips of flesh. Rotten blood filled his mouth and Apep howled with pain.

Typhoon tore off one of Apep's legs; it grew back, like some sick thing being born out of the blood pouring from his arm. He howled as he punched Typhoon in the ribs, sending him skittering back several steps. A good two dozen vampires swarmed in, separating him from Apep. He fought, but there was no way he was getting through them any time soon.

So, it's all up to me. Daniel took a moment to catch his breath, waiting to see if Apep was going to send vampires after him, too. None of them moved toward him, satisfying themselves with trying to get to Gracie now; she was still tearing through those invisible chains. The vampires she had already freed turned against Apep's forces, defending her while shouting their hatred at Apep.

The god snarled as he lunged for her, as though Daniel was utterly unimportant. Daniel threw himself forward, intercepting them. He caught Apep by the shoulder and yanked him backward, bones snapping in his jaws as he did so. Apep's clawed hand swiped at his face and he jumped to one side, then rushed in and grabbed his wrist. He shook and jerked, snapping the arm and yanking it out of the shoulder socket. Apep howled with pain; Daniel's hope rang true as the broken bone healed at an awkward angle that made it next to useless.

With a snarl, he whipped around and punched Daniel in the face. As Daniel tried to dodge it, he kicked him full in the ribs. Daniel heard something snap as he was thrown into the stone wall. Darkness washed over his head and every breath he drew hurt, but he stumbled back to his feet, shaking himself as he panted, glaring at Apep.

Apep wrenched his arm, snapping it back, and shoved it back into place. He wiped his mouth and, ignoring Daniel once more, went straight for Gracie. A large group of vampires turned to attack Daniel, and Gracie let out a shout. A burst of light flooded out from her, and all the vampires in the vicinity shouted, covering their eyes and cringed away from her. Even Apep.

Daniel didn't waste time. He leapt onto Apep's back, tearing at the back of his neck. Apep let out a howl, slamming himself and Daniel both against the wall. Something else cracked and Daniel clawed at Apep, trying to free himself.

The light around Gracie increased until Daniel could see thin beams of red, surrounding Apep and reaching out to ensnare other vampires. Gracie's hands wrapped around them, snapping the beams as Apep howled once more. He elbowed Daniel in the gut and went for Gracie again. Daniel's leg wasn't working properly, making him stumble as he tried to chase after Apep.

A dozen of the vampires who had been attacking Typhoon turned and leapt at Apep. He punched his way through them, then waded through Gracie's protectors and seized her about the shoulders. Daniel howled, throwing himself forward. Once more, Gracie was pulled from Apep's grip. Daniel tore into Apep's neck as the red bands around him grew thinner and thinner until they all snapped.

Apep collapsed to his knees as Typhoon darted in, grabbing him by the arm and holding him in place for Daniel to tear into his abdomen. Apep roared, lashing out with his free hand. Teeth tore into Daniel's flank even as the scent of death filled the air. Darkness washed in and out of his vision. The screams seemed to echo in his skull, but he didn't stop, digging and tearing.

Typhoon's jaws clenched over Apep's head and Daniel was able to get a good grip on Apep's throat. They tore together as Apep's arms crushed around his chest. Spurts of blood splashed in his eyes as he and Typhoon tore together, ripping Apep's head clean from his body.

The headless corpse thrashed; they didn't stop, continuing to tear and rip until Apep was scattered in a hundred pieces.

When Daniel finally backed away, panting, he promptly collapsed. Pain washed through him from his multiple wounds and he could taste his own blood on his tongue, mingled with the rotten stink of Apep. He heard his name and limply rose his head to see Gracie rush to him.

All around them, vampires stood in a wide circle. Many embraced each other, sobbing. A few still fought weakly, and a handful were on their knees, wailing Apep's name. Most, however, silently got to their knees as Typhoon shifted back to his human form, Apep's black blood staining his skin. He glared out over them as the shifters made their way to stand with him.

Gracie's arms wrapped around Daniel's body and he licked her face. He just needed to rest...

"We won't kill any more of you than necessary," he spat out. "If you don't fight us, then there will be no need for us to kill you."

From nearby, one of the vampires got to his feet again and stepped forward. Tears streaked down his face. "You killed Apep and freed us from him. We... we never thought shifters would..."

Guinevere, with Andy beside her, joined Typhoon. "There has been enough bloodshed. Enough pain, enough of us fighting each other."

Daniel grunted as he pushed himself to his knees and slowly shifted back to human form. His ribs ached like a motherfucker and his leg was bent at the wrong angle, but he was able to pull in deeper breaths now, and with Gracie's help got to his feet. Her eyes shone with tears, and he would have kissed her but for the disgusting stuff still in his mouth. He spat out a mouthful of Apep's blood and limped to join his parents and Typhoon.

"I'm proof that shifters and vampires don't have to hate each other," he called to the gathered vampires. "And my mate, Gracie, can remove the chains of your bloodlust. You'll be able to live your lives without fear of losing control. She's already broken the bloodlust in many of you. She is a daughter of Ra and can give you what Apep tried to ensure you would never have."

Gracie straightened a little. "I am a child of Ra," she agreed, her voice calm and strong. "But I am no goddess, nor do I want to be one. I will take away the bloodlust if you'll let me... But as Typhoon and Guinevere have said, enough is enough. Humans know about vampires now, and we have proof that vampires and shifters can live in peace. So will you? Will you choose peace? Or will you choose death?"

Chapter Sixteen

Gracie

Five Months Later

Gracie nuzzled into Daniel's neck, her hands moving down his shirt to undo buttons. His tongue flicked over her jaw, sending pleasant tingles through her. Gracie sighed as she slid her hands into his open shirt, enjoying the warmth of his smooth, taut skin. She smiled at him and he smiled back, his hand running up her thigh.

Her core tightened, making her shiver, as his fingers massaged her through her damp underwear. They returned to each other's mouths, kissing and nibbling on each other's lips while Gracie continued to undress them both. She undid his jeans, her movements a little jerky in her haste, and they both laughed a little at her eagerness.

"You can slow down," Daniel crooned. "We have lots of time."

Gracie sniffed the air. "We have a visitor… do we really have a lot of time?"

Daniel grimaced. "He can wait."

"I couldn't agree more."

Gracie bucked her hips upward, moving one of her hands to Daniel's shoulder, encouraging him to roll over and lay on his back. She took him in her hand, kissing down his open shirt as she stroked him evenly. He let out a grunt, his hips rocking in time with her movements as his eyes slid half-closed. Gracie couldn't help but laugh a little at that. She always loved the way he looked when she pleasured him. As though she was the only person to have ever given him this. Warmth spread through her chest as she considered that he was hers, just as much as she was his. And they would be together forever.

"I love you," she whispered as she bent over him, taking him into her mouth.

His reply was garbled with a grunt. His hands dug into the bedding as she sucked on him with the pressure she knew he liked. As she watched him, moving her head to make him hard and ready, the tightness inside of her tingled. She knew exactly what she wanted today. It was something that Daniel had hinted at wanting, but he was such a gentleman that he never stated it outright; she knew he was waiting for her to make the move.

And as she sucked on him, loving the taste of him, letting her fangs gently scrape against his skin, she reached between her thighs. Her underwear were more than damp by this time, and she played with her clit, teasing herself until it was as hard and swollen as Daniel was.

When he was on edge and trembling, ready to release, he put a hand on her shoulder and gently encouraged her to back up. He took a moment to regain control of himself, then gestured for her to lie back.

"My turn."

"Yes," Gracie agreed. "But not like that." Daniel arched a brow, and she giggled, nervous about what she was about to do. "You know how I went shopping earlier?"

Daniel nodded.

"Well, I got something… special."

"Okay…"

Gracie waited a moment, her eyes dancing, as Daniel peered at her suspiciously. Her heart hammered against her chest as she bounced over to the nightstand and opened it up to withdraw the treasures she had purchased earlier. First was a bottle of lube, then a roll of condoms, and finally a small pamphlet, which she waved in front of Daniel's face before setting it down with the other stuff.

Daniel picked up the condoms. "We don't use these."

His eyes widened when he picked up the pamphlet. A sly grin crossed his face as he reached over to her, sliding one hand between her thighs to toy with her clit, the other reaching around her to grasp her ass. "Anal sex for beginners? Are you sure?"

A shiver ran through her as his fingers toyed with her clit. She had to grasp his shoulder to keep herself upright as she nodded, letting out a soft moan while her eyes slid shut.

"I've been thinking about it. We use toys in my ass all the time... I'm ready to take it to the next level."

Daniel let out a groan as he turned her around. He yanked her underwear off and squished her ass with his hands, fingers digging into her soft flesh. He rubbed himself over her ass, and Gracie's skin nearly burst into flame. She held onto the wall, bracing herself while he buried his face into her neck, licking and nuzzling her until she was nearly screaming with impatience; one hand continued to work at her clit and she trembled with need.

"Ready?" Daniel breathed, moving them both back to the bed.

Gracie could only moan to let him know she was. She bent over the bed, offering her ass to him and hid her face in the blankets. Very, very gently, Daniel pulled on a condom and applied a generous amount of lube on himself, then her ass; he used his fingers to open her up and get plenty inside of her before oh so slowly pushing himself into her. The pressure from his size made her groan, but with one hand still on her clit, it was all she could do to stay still.

"Gently," she whispered, though she knew he wouldn't need to be told.

He kissed her back, making her shiver again, and then slowly began to move.

It was different than what Gracie expected; they had to move slowly, and even as the fires spread throughout her body, making her gasp and moan, Daniel didn't release any of his control. He kept his thrusts even, grunting every now and then but always keeping up his strokes on her clit. It was all so intense that when her core exploded, making her writhe with pleasure and a scream echo from her throat, she didn't even feel him finish.

Daniel fell over her, kissing and biting at her shoulders until they were both too tired to move. Then, he eased himself out gently and held her tight while they panted for breath.

After some time, Daniel moaned in disappointment. “He’s still here.”

Gracie sniffed the air again and sighed. Typhoon’s scent was still strong, coming from the hallway where he’d been waiting for some time already. She wondered if he hadn’t knocked out of respect for their privacy; then she wondered if he had knocked and they just hadn’t heard it. She giggled a little at that thought, then sighed as she rolled over. She was a little sore from their first time having sex that way, but not as bad as she thought it would be... while they were having sex, she hadn’t felt any pain at all.

Which she was glad for. She drank enough shifter blood that these days she was almost completely human, and healing took a lot longer than it did when she was a vampire.

"We better see what he wants," Daniel grumbled.

Gracie nodded her agreement. They took their time dressing, half hoping that Typhoon would leave before they were ready. He wasn't, though, and gave them a knowing smile when they finally opened the door. Gracie retrieved some beers for the three of them. Honestly, it would be nice when she and Daniel finally had a week to themselves.

The last five months had been a lot of work. For starters, she had been kept busy removing the bloodlust from the vampires. There were so many of them that it was a full-time job. After that, it was a matter of working out new alliances and helping humans rebuild their governments while the vampires figured out what they were going to do from here on out.

"I trust you're both doing well?" Typhoon said as he sat, accepting the beer handed to him.

"Yeah," Daniel replied with a nod. "If we can get any time to ourselves."

A smile twisted Typhoon's lips. "You wanted to be an alpha. And when you're an alpha, you don't get a lot of time for yourself."

Gracie sighed at that. She knew it was true, and with her trying to figure out her position with the vampires, too, it meant that they weren't going to be getting their uninterrupted week anytime soon. She sat next to Daniel, putting her arm around his waist. It was something that she would have to get used to... but being with her mate made it all worth it.

Typhoon lifted his beer and peered at it for a moment before chugging a large mouthful and putting it down. “I’m here to discuss the leadership of the Savage Brotherhood.”

“Hey, everybody was happy to have you back as the alpha.” Daniel held up a hand. “And I know I have a lot left to learn. So, if you’re worried about me trying to take over—”

“Just the opposite, in fact.” Typhoon grinned broadly. “I’m going to retire.”

Gracie’s eyes widened, and Daniel’s jaw dropped.

“With the vampires integrating with humans, no longer having to fight the desire for blood to the point of murder,” here he nodded at Gracie, “they are free to choose their own destinies. And with that, most of them are no longer choosing to live a life underground. They want to have lives again... they want to be able to make up to humans what Apep forced them to do."

"Yes, but—" Daniel started.

"For my whole life," Typhoon interrupted, "I've hated vampires. I've hated myself for being half vampire. The Savage Brotherhood has a different role now. We will no longer be fighting the vampires, no longer defending humans against them. Now we have to be mediators. Helping humans, shifters, and vampires to find a way to live in peace. I am far too biased to be a good candidate for that role."

Gracie took Daniel's hand, finally understanding what Typhoon was meaning. "So, you want Daniel to do it."

Typhoon nodded.

"Well... thank you for the vote of confidence but I—"

"You're ready. You fought against Apep. You reunited a shattered Brotherhood." Typhoon grinned at him. "And you have a pretty remarkable mate. You are more than ready for his, Daniel. And I am more than ready to retire and settle down with my mate and child. The future is bright, and you will make it even brighter. Of that, I'm positive."

Gracie and Daniel glanced at one another. There was a question in Daniel's eyes, but there was no hesitation from Gracie as she nodded.

Typhoon was right. Daniel was ready, and he was the best choice for moving forward. One of the things about him growing up so rapidly was that he hadn't had the years to grow jaded like Typhoon or others were.

She squeezed his hand and her grin widened. Daniel smiled back, then nodded at Typhoon. "Let's do this, then. I'm ready."

*****

THE END

16263273R00152

Printed in Great Britain
by Amazon